Murder
in Babylon

Other Books by Michael B. Druxman

Fiction

Dracula Meets Jack The Ripper & Other Revisionist Histories
Once Upon A Time In Hollywood: From the Secret Files of Harry
    Pennypacker
Shadow Watcher
Nobody Drowns In Mineral Lake

Non-Fiction

Life, Liberty & The Pursit of Hollywood
My Forty-Five Years In Hollywood And How I Escaped Alive
Family Secret (with Warren Hull)
The Art of Storytelling
The Musical: From Broadway To Hollywood
One Good Film Deserves Another
Charlton Heston
Merv
Make It Again, Sam
Basil Rathbone: His Life and His Films
Paul Muni: His Life And His Films

Stage Plays (*The Hollywood Legends*)

B Movie
Clara Bow
Chevalier
Flynn
Gable
Jolson
Lombard
Nelson and Jeanette
Rathbone
Tracy
Orson Welles

Other Stage Plays

Hail on the Chief!
Putz
The Summer Folk

Screenplays

The Amusement	Barry & The Bimbo
Black Watch / The Cavern	Charla
Cheyenne Warrior	Cheyenne Warrior II / Hawk
Ghoul City	Matricide
Ride Along	Sarah Golden Hair
The Summer Folk	Uncle Louie

MURDER
IN BABYLON

A Novel
Based
on Fact

Michael B. Druxman

BearManor Media

2015

Murder In Babylon: A Novel Based on Fact
© 2015 Michael B. Druxman

For information, address:

BearManor Media
P. O. Box 71426
Albany, GA 31708

bearmanormedia.com

Typesetting and layout by John Teehan

Published in the USA by BearManor Media

ISBN—1-59393-782-2
978-1-59393-782-9

In memory of William Desmond Taylor.
Would anybody really know his name today
had he not been murdered?
R.I.P.

Acknowledgments

Special thanks to Adela Rogers St. Johns and King Vidor for giving me the inside scoop; helping me separate fact from rumor in this nearly century old case.

Prologue

EDITORIAL

Last weekend's appointment of Postmaster General Will H. Hayes to head the Motion Picture Producers and Distributors Association is a move that will be applauded by all Americans concerned with the preservation of this nation's basic liberties.

Even before the sordid Arbuckle murder scandal broke last September, the motion picture industry had been facing the specter of national censorship. Churches and reform groups had long objected to films featuring, as one advertisement put it, "beautiful jazz babies, champagne baths, midnight revels, petting parties in the purple dawn, all ending in one terrific smashing climax that makes you gasp".

Labeling the Hollywood community a "modern-day Babylon", these mid-west and eastern reform societies are now securing pledges from Congressmen who are coming up for re-election, binding them to support a national censorship measure. There is a campaign now planned which is the largest in scope since that which brought about Prohibition. To launch that campaign, an upcoming Sunday has been chosen and on that day, every pulpit in the nation will be the scene of the unleashing of an attack on the motion picture industry.

1

Whereas The Dispatch *believes that moral restraint should be exercised both on the screen and in the public private lives of some of its more trouble-prone personalities, we vigorously object to the proposals now being set forth.*

Censorship is a dangerous weapon that can easily be misused. Today we may only outlaw certain pictures, but, once unleashed, this power may next turn its attention to books of controversy or even objectionable ideas in the press.

The frightened film leaders have shown great wisdom in drafting Mr. Hays out of President Harding's cabinet. It is our belief that he will be able to give this adolescent industry the moral guidance it requires to "clean its own house" and thereby avoid the threatened national sanctions.

– from the *Los Angeles Dispatch*
January 18, 1922

A warm smile greeted the banjo-eyed beauty as she swept into the bank manager's office. It was her monthly visit to pick up cancelled checks and leave her checkbook for balancing. She never seemed to be able to keep those damn numbers straight herself and, since the staff at the Hellman Bank didn't object to handling this extra chore, she always made it a point to let them sort out that monthly mess. It was one of the advantages of being a movie star.

A bit of small talk with the balding official, then away to entrust a diamond bracelet to her safety deposit box.

It had been a busy day—a trip to the jeweler, an extended session with Marjorie Berger, her tax advisor, and finally, these errands at the bank. She was tired. Maybe she'd catch Harold Lloyd's new film while she was downtown, and then go home to an early bedtime. After all, she had a seven o'clock call at the studio tomorrow.

Halfway to the exit, she decided she'd better call home for messages. The girl at the new accounts counter gladly surrendered the use of her phone.

Mamie Owens, her maid, answered on the second ring. "Mr. Taylor has called three or four times," she reported. "He sent over a book from Parker's and said to tell you he'd stopped at Robinson's and picked up another book you wanted. He said you should come by his place on your way home and get it."

The air had turned cold when Mabel Normand – screen comedienne extraordinaire – emerged from the bank late that February 1st afternoon and hurried to her waiting Rolls. She told William Davis, her chauffer, that she'd decided to skip the movie and, instead, he should take her to Mr. Taylor's home on Alvarado.

Mabel felt good as she was driven down Main Street amid a surge of pedestrians rushing to complete their chores before the business day ended. Her health was better than it had been in some time; her new film, *Molly O*, had started to garner an impressive box-office; and, most important, she was on her way to visit with Bill Taylor.

The tall, cultured film director was unlike any man she had ever known. In the year since they'd met through actress Edna Purviance at a Hollywood gathering, Mabel had grown quite fond of this handsome British import. Perhaps they'd marry someday. He certainly cared for her - tried to help her overcome the damaging physical need she'd been expensively feeding for some time - and he'd proposed.

But, damn it, Sennett, that son-of-a-bitch, kept working his way back into her life and, after so many years, she couldn't dismiss him from her emotions that easily.

What baffled Mabel was why Bill was interested in her in the first place. True, she was a talented big movie star, had a great figure, beautiful black hair, dressed well (those Paris designers could retire on what she paid for her wardrobe), and, maybe, she was fun to be with. But, Christ, Bill Taylor could find fifty actresses in this town with those same qualifications - and brains to match. Hell, she couldn't even read to herself without moving her lips.

Not that she was stupid. She just wasn't a "lady." She didn't possess that innate "style" or "class" she'd envied in so many of her contemporaries. Face it; she was an attractive, good-natured "schnook." What else could one expect from a poor French/Irish girl from Staten Island?

Bill Taylor, that wonderful guy, had taken her under his wing. He tolerated her crazy stunts and wild fits of temper, gave her good books to read, introduced her to the world of art, and spent hours with her discussing literature and the finer things in life.

Maybe she was worrying about it too much.

She had Davis stop at the Pacific Electric Building, so she could buy a bag of peanuts from the sidewalk vendor. When he didn't have change for a twenty, she went inside to the newsstand where she purchased the *Police Gazette* and noted the headline on the *Los Angeles Dispatch*, which announced that the second Fatty Arbuckle manslaughter trial was drawing to a close.

That whole business was just too disgusting to read about today. Roscoe Arbuckle, her former co-star at Keystone, was a friend - a good friend. She couldn't believe that he was responsible for that girl's death in San Francisco last fall. Yet, the newspapers and the "do-gooders" were using him as the symbol for all the supposed sin and wickedness that was taking place in Hollywood these days. At least, that's the way that Bill had put it.

She gathered up her change, her *Police Gazette*, and the new *Photoplay*, then got her peanuts from the vendor outside and returned to her automobile. Nibbling her snack, she settled back to enjoy her favorite reading matter as she was chauffeured to 404-B South Alvarado Street.

It was almost seven o'clock when the limousine arrived at the exclusive bungalow court in which Taylor resided. The two-story Spanish-style duplexes, which were located kiddy-corner to Westlake Park, housed several of filmdom's most prominent personalities.

Stepping from the car, Mabel instructed Davis to clean up the shells that were scattered over the floor. The chauffer forced a weak smile while his mistress, still carrying both the bag of nuts and her cancelled checks, headed for the director's cottage.

Henry Peavey, a lanky Negro dressed in yellow knickers and a dark coat, answered the door. Mabel tried to avoid chuckling at the houseman's unorthodox attire. "Good evening, Henry. Is Mr. Taylor at home?"

"Yes, 'um,'" was the high-pitched reply. "He's talkin' on the telephone."

As she walked into the entry hall, Mabel recognized Bill's precise, usually soft-spoken voice coming from under the stairs. Evidently, he was somewhat agitated with his caller.

Not wishing to eavesdrop, the actress turned to the servant. "That was a delicious pudding you prepared last night, Henry. Mr. Taylor and I finished the whole thing."

Peavey knew she was referring to his custard that had sat uneaten in the icebox for two days. He'd found the empty tin in the sink when he'd come to work that morning. "Thank you, ma'am. I wondered who'd been here after I left."

Mabel smiled, then, realizing that the director had finished his call, shifted her attention to the alcove.

William Desmond Taylor rushed out to meet his waiting guest. Taking her hands in his, no small task insofar as she was still grasping the sack of peanuts, the checks and her oversized handbag, the slightly graying model of British elegance escorted her into his photograph-lined living room.

At forty-nine, Taylor had developed an enviable talent for dealing with women. His distinguished features, coupled with gentlemanly charm and impeccable taste in clothing, made him one of the most popular bachelors in the Hollywood community.

"You must be working on your taxes, too," remarked Mabel, noticing the open checkbook and clutter of forms on the mahogany desk.

"That and, of course, it's the first of the month. I've just been going over some matters with Marjorie Berger."

"Really? I just left her."

Mabel collapsed on the large tapestry divan. "I am so bloody tired," she said. "Making movies is fuckin' goddamned easier than all the rushing around that I've done today."

Taylor had come to accept his guest's colorful vocabulary. He picked up a volume from the desk and walked over to sit next to her. "Here's the book you came for. I think you'll find it interesting."

The work was by Sigmund Freud – a bit deep for Miss Normand, but one that she wanted to read to please Taylor. "Good," she said. "I hear it's pretty risqué."

Peavey came in to serve cocktails.

"Stay for dinner?" asked Taylor.

"No, you've already eaten," replied Mabel, pointing to the dirty dishes on the table in the adjoining dining room. "Besides, I want to go to bed early and you've got work to do."

Peavey inquired, "Will you need me anymore this evening, Mr. Taylor?"

"I don't think so, Henry. Just clean up the dining room and you can go."

The couple discussed Freud loosely for the next few minutes while Peavey finished his chores and departed.

"Poor Henry," said Taylor. "He's worried about tomorrow."

"Oh, that court thing is tomorrow, isn't it," remembered Mabel. "You ought to let Peavey play golf more often, so he won't get into trouble at the park."

Taylor laughed at her reference to Peavey's outfit. "I really don't know why he's dressed that way. I only hope he wears something more conservative when we're at the City Prosecutor's."

"What *did* he do?"

"I don't know all the details, but, as I understand it, it's an indecent exposure charge and there was a young boy involved. Perhaps I should discharge him. And yet, he's such a good houseman that I don't think I could find anyone better."

"Maybe Sands would come back," said Mabel with a knowing smile.

"Please," sighed Taylor, not appreciating her humor. "If I could get my hands on Sands, I'd kill him.

"Part of the problem I'm having with my taxes right now has to do with the checks he forged. I can't tell which are mine and which are his."

Edward F. Sands had been Taylor's valet who, during the director's journey to England some months before, had burglarized his home of all its valuables and forged a number of checks. In recent weeks, the stocky man had allegedly broken into the house on two additional occasions and Taylor had sworn out a warrant for his arrest.

Mabel noticed that it was almost 7:45 and informed her host that she must be getting home. Disappointed that she was departing, but always gallant, he planted an affectionate kiss on her lips. They walked, arm-in-arm, back to her waiting auto.

"I'll try to start Mr. Freud in bed tonight," said Mabel, as Taylor handed over her small parcels.

He pointed to the *Police Gazette* on the seat beside her. "Good Lord, Mabel, you're going in for terrible literature this year."

She gave him a sheepish grin.

"Can I stop over later?" he asked.

"Well, yes, if I have my dinner downstairs. If I don't, I'm going upstairs and have a bath and go to bed, and I promise you I'll be asleep. But, call about nine o'clock anyway."

"Nine o'clock," repeated Taylor, blowing her a kiss.

Davis put the car in gear. A U-turn headed it down Alvarado toward Wilshire.

Mabel hoped she could stay awake for the promised call that evening, though she doubted if she'd be alert enough to see Bill again.

Cold from the biting night air, Taylor watched the limousine speed away, then hurried back into the court and through the front door he'd left open.

It was a few minutes before the shot was fired.

Henry Peavey, dressed in his best clothes, was in a state of near panic when he arrived at work Thursday morning. He knew he was goin' to jail. He'd done a terrible thing and he just knew he was goin' to be punished.

Damn, he was dumb to have pulled his pecker out in front of that boy in the park. He shouldn't have had so much to drink that afternoon. *That's* what made him do it.

He weren't such a bad guy. It weren't his fault he liked little boys. He was born that way.

Well, maybe Mr. Taylor could help him. Mr. Taylor was an important man. He'd talk to the police... or whoever they had to see today... and maybe they'd go easy on him. Oh, Lord, he hoped so. He truly hoped so.

The houseman's watch read 7:30 a.m. when he inserted the key into Taylor's front door and turned the latch.

He saw the body almost immediately. It was resting on the mulberry velvet carpet just inside the living room. The arms were neatly at its sides and the face, though ashen, was perfectly composed. Lying on top of the feet was an overturned chair.

Peavey bolted from the house. "Oh, Lord! Oh, my God!" he screamed, running up and down the court, "Mr. Taylor's dead! Help! Mr. Taylor's dead in the front room!"

The Negro's shrill voice quickly woke the sleeping neighbors. In robe and slippers, screen comedian Douglas MacLean and his pretty wife, Faith, emerged from their residence, located right across the court from the late director's, and attempted to understand what the frightened man was saying.

E.C. Jessurum, the elderly owner of the apartments, hurried out of his quarters while still pulling his robe around him. Taking hold of the houseman, he commanded, "Calm down, Henry. Take it easy and tell me what happened."

Peavey, unable to contain his emotions, blurted through the tears, "Mr. Taylor is dead! He's *dead!*"

The director's closest neighbor, Edna Purviance, stuck her head out the door to see what had awakened her at such an "ungodly" hour. It had been one o'clock before the blonde and lovely leading lady for Charlie Chaplin went to bed that night.

Billy Taylor dead? My God! That was impossible! After all, she'd just seen him yesterday morning. And last night, when she'd got home around midnight after that late supper, his light had been on. She'd even knocked at the door to see if he wanted to chat for a while. Then, when he didn't answer, figured he was entertaining some sweet young thing in the bedroom.

Jesus, with Billy dead, strangers would be going through his things, and that could be embarrassing for a lot of people.

Edna decided that she'd better make some phone calls.

Howard Fellows, Taylor's chauffer, had arrived at the scene to take his employer to the studio that morning. He stopped Douglas MacLean, who was rushing into the street to summon a doctor.

"What's going on?" asked the baffled young man.

"Your boss is dead," snapped the slender, pixyish comedian, as he ran by.

Fellows moved slowly up to the open door of the cottage, saw the body, then headed straight for the alcove under the stairs and the telephone.

Another neighbor, Mrs. Verne Duma, peered out her upstairs window, learned of the death, and thought it might be a good idea if somebody phoned for the police.

The sharp scream of the phone woke Mabel Normand from her sound sleep. Assuming it was Bill Taylor with his nine o'clock call, she reached out for the receiver.

"Mabel?"

"Yes," she yawned.

"This is Edna. Billy Taylor's valet is running around the court here shouting that Bill's dead."

The news confused the actress. "What time is it?"

"About 7:45."

Mabel realized that she'd slept through the night. Without saying goodbye to Edna, she replaced the receiver and struggled to comprehend what she'd just heard.

The news of Bill's passing was crushing, but more important than that, she was worried about those goddamn letters.

Charles Eyton had just arrived in his office at the Famous Players-Lasky lot when his secretary told him that Harry Fellows, Taylor's assistant director, was on the line. The heavy-set studio manager considered passing on the call until after he'd read the morning paper, but since Fellows seldom phoned his office, he assumed it must be something important.

"Mr. Eyton," Fellows said, "my brother, Howard, just phoned me. He says that Bill Taylor's dead. He's lying in his living room and it looks like he had a heart attack."

"Shit!"

"What was that?" asked the bewildered Fellows.

Eyton remembered that he was no longer a sports promoter and that he shouldn't make slips like that. "Harry," he said, "I want you to meet me over at Taylor's right away." He slammed down the phone and headed out the door. Pausing momentarily, he instructed his secretary, "Call Ted Taylor in publicity. Tell him that Bill Taylor's dead. He'll know what to do."

The studio boss had to get to Taylor's bungalow before the press. Christ, his bosses would kill him if he didn't. That's all this studio needed was another scandal.

That damn woman scenario writer who killed herself last spring… Why did one of the Famous Players executives have to be fucking her? Well, he'd been able to keep that one fairly quiet as far as the press was concerned, but the rumors wouldn't quit.

He could do nothing with the Arbuckle mess. Three finished pictures starring that fat bastard were in the can and he had to go get himself involved in the biggest murder scandal of the decade.

And now, Bill Taylor. Hell, he was quite an asset to the studio, at least from the public relations standpoint - President of the Director's Association and all that class. He was really great for impressing the out-of-town muckrakers that were trying to destroy the industry. The studio got more good copy in the east by way of Taylor's charm than through any of the contract stars.

Eyton smiled to himself as he climbed into his waiting limousine. On the other hand, he wasn't too unhappy about the English son-of-a-bitch's passing after all.

The executive's automobile departed the Sunset and Vine lot, heading for South Alvarado Street.

"The lonely princess" wasn't at home when Edna Purviance called. Her mother, Charlotte Shelby, answered the phone. Edna didn't particularly like this cold-eyed matron who kept her somewhat talented daughter caged like a prize show dog. In fact, nobody in the film industry did much more than tolerate the mother of Mary Miles

Minter.

As Edna understood the situation, the red-headed Mrs. Shelby had deserted her husband, a printer from Dallas, when her two daughters were still quite young. She took the girls to New York where it was her idea to fulfill her lifelong ambition of becoming a famous stage actress. However, things did not go quite as planned for her and, although she'd been able to secure some small roles, it seemed that producers were more interested in utilizing the talents of her charming six-year-old daughter, Juliet.

An astute businesswoman, Mrs. Shelby soon realized that managing her youngest daughter's career could prove more profitable than pursuing her own, so over the next few years, she'd done just that and "Little Juliet Shelby" became the reigning child star of the American Theatre. Edna recalled that a few years back the girl had played with the Farnum brothers in *The Littlest Rebel*.

Chaplin's favorite comedienne wasn't too clear on how "Little Juliet Shelby" became Mary Miles Minter, but she did know that the reason for the change had something to do with child labor laws that threatened to prevent the girl from performing in a large city. In any case, the Shelby's finally arrived in Los Angeles. Mary Miles Minter became Mary Pickford's closest rival for the "sweet young thing" roles and was, eventually, contracted by Famous Players to fill those assignments after Miss Pickford had departed for greener pastures.

Mary Miles Minter was one of the town's biggest stars and, though on the shy side, a sweet girl to be around. Perhaps that was why she accepted the abusive treatment her mother and aggressive, less talented sister, Margaret, chose to dole out to her. Edna couldn't think of any other reason why the almost adult Mary allowed her family to treat her like a child of eight or nine – forcing her to maintain her long curls, wear Mary Janes and other clothing styles that belonged on a girl years younger, and, most interesting, refusing to entrust more than a couple dollars of her four-figure salary to her. Whereas Margaret dated, played in the sun and, in general, led a normal life, Mary was sheltered, lest a little fun erode her bread-winning capabilities.

Even Edna could appreciate that Mary had been deeply hurt growing up lacking a father and that was probably the reason she'd been attracted to her director, Bill Taylor. Her mother would deny the truth of that, but Edna, as well as most of the Hollywood community, knew what had been going on in Taylor's bungalow.

On this frantic morning, the sensitive Miss Purviance was in no mood to have "words" with Charlotte Shelby. Taking the easy way out, she delivered the bad news to Mama and hoped that the parent would pass it on to her daughter with a certain gentleness that had always seemed missing from her character.

The pretty blonde little girl of nineteen spotted her mother's Packard pulling into the driveway from her upstairs bedroom window. Not wishing to repeat the fight that had caused her to flee the house last night, Mary Miles Minter ran to the door and locked it.

Here, at the home of her widowed grandmother, Julia Miles, Mary found her only refuge. Utilizing what little influence she had on her daughter, the domineering Charlotte, Mrs. Miles attempted to garner for the fragile Mary as many privileges as possible. It seemed to the reluctant actress that, while at her grandmother's, she also got along better with her sister, Margaret, and so she welcomed these overnight visits.

She heard the downstairs door slam, but was unable to understand what her excited mother was shouting about. Moments later, Mrs. Shelby was pounding on the bedroom door. "Open the door," she demanded. "I've something to tell you."

Some procrastination, then the obedient girl turned the latch.

Eyton arrived at the Alvarado Street bungalow to find Harry Fellows already there, instructing his brother to keep the curious pajama-clad court residents away from the dead director's door. The site had, obviously, had its share of "tourists." Spotting the studio manager, Harry motioned for him to retreat out onto the sidewalk so they could escape the ears of uninvited listeners.

"Doug MacLean's in the house now with a doctor," reported the assistant director. "Evidently, two policemen were here, but they left."

"What killed him?"

"I don't know yet, but from the look of him, it must have been natural causes. He seems so peaceful lying there."

"Let's go see the doctor," said Eyton, reentering the court.

The physician had just completed his cursory examination of the body when the men entered the room. They interrupted MacLean, who was showing him the location of the telephone.

"Doctor, I'm Charles Eyton," announced the executive, attempting to appear grief-stricken. "I run the studio where Mr. Taylor was employed."

The medical man, middle-aged with a pencil-thin mustache, nodded for him to state his business.

"Can you tell me the cause of death?"

"He died of a gastric hemorrhage," said the doctor, indicating a small brown bloodstain in the corner of Taylor's mouth. "He probably had a perforated ulcer."

Eyton thanked the physician, who then phoned the coroner's office and promptly departed to fulfill his other duties. MacLean started to leave also, but was stopped by the studio manager. "Doug," confided Eyton, "I wonder if we can count on you."

"In what way?"

"I'm sure you realize that it wouldn't help the image of the film industry if some of the details of Bill's private life got into the papers. Those scandal sheets would have nothing but fun with the story and a lot of innocent people would be hurt."

The comic was well aware of the sensational accounts the press was printing about the Arbuckle case, so he knew exactly what Eyton meant. "What can I do?" he asked.

His confederate enlisted, the studio manager put his plan into action. "Why don't you take Bill's supply of liquor over to your house and just keep it. We don't need to give the Prohibitionists something to yell about."

With MacLean occupied by his assignment, Eyton turned to Harry, who was staring at the body, trying to let the reality of the situation penetrate. "Fellows, I want to go through the house rather quickly, get anything out of here that can prove embarrassing. You check upstairs. Look for papers, letters, anything you think shouldn't get into the wrong hands. And check the medicine cabinet."

The assistant got busy, while his boss headed for Taylor's desk to do the same job.

It was a few minutes before Fellows was back downstairs. He flashed a bundle of letters at Eyton, just finishing at the desk, when the assistant coroner entered, followed by a team of ambulance attendants bearing a stretcher. Harry quickly pocketed his find.

Eyton took over the situation – introducing both himself and Fellows – then instructed his nervous associate to meet him back at the studio.

"The doctor who was here a while ago said it was a gastric hemorrhage," offered Eyton.

Impressed with meeting a man of the executive's stature, the youngish official nodded in agreement and indicated that his companions should remove the corpse.

The blood oozing from the director's back had dyed the soft carpet beneath the body a deeper hue of red. Eyton blanched at the sight.

"He's been shot," said the startled representative from the coroner's office.

THE WILLIAM DESMOND TAYLOR CASE

A Memoir by
Benjamin A. Birnbaum

On February 22, 1922, I was a veteran reporter of twenty-seven with the old *Los Angeles Dispatch*. I'd started with the paper as a copy boy three years earlier. Ninety days after that, I was writing obituaries and, in less than a year, I was covering major news events. True, the biggest stories—like the sensational Madalyne Obenchain murder trial—usually went to the staff reporters with the most tenure, but I got my fair share of interesting assignments.

Aside from my relative youth, which I, unsuccessfully, tried to hide by nursing a mustache and smoking a pipe, I had another handicap working against me getting the top jobs. I'm an Orthodox Jew and, come what may, I quit work at sundown on Friday nights to observe the Sabbath. There could be another San Francisco earthquake, but if it occurred on the Sabbath or one of the Holy Days, somebody else would have to cover it. I don't even answer my phone on those days.

Naturally, this attitude became a constant source of displeasure for my Irish city editor, Andrew Lundy, who seemed to be always begging me to make an exception "just this one time". Lundy was a good newspaperman, actually one of the best: a cocky, little, hard-drinking guy with red hair, and the owner of the most outlandish green-striped suspenders I've ever seen.

Old Andy and I actually got along pretty well, mainly because he knew that I could get the story. He came to respect my religious beliefs and, aside from an occasional argument over the work schedule, they never interfered with our relationship, which says a lot for the man since anti-Semitic prejudice was quite common back in the twenties.

If it hadn't been for the influenza epidemic that seemed to be bedding half of Los Angeles, including much of our editorial staff, in the early days of 1922, I probably never would have drawn the William Desmond Taylor story.

I was helping out on the rewrite desk when Ted Taylor (no relation) from the publicity department at Famous Players-Lasky (now known as Paramount) phoned in around eight in the morning to tell us that William Desmond Taylor, the studio's top director (after Cecil B. DeMille), had been found dead at 404-B South Alvarado Street. Cause of death appeared to be a gastric hemorrhage.

Reading with some difficulty from a prepared studio biography, publicist Taylor filled me in on the director's background so that I could write an obituary:

The late Mr. Taylor had been born fifty-five years earlier (the death certificate would reveal he was almost fifty) *in Mallows, County Cork, Ireland. His mother was Irish and his father was a colonel in the British Army. His father had hoped that his son would enter the army and sent him to Clifton College in England for preparatory work in engineering. Before his military examination, he was disqualified from service because of eye trouble. He then went to France and Germany for further engineering study.*

At the age of eighteen, he entered the theatrical profession by taking a small part in Charles Hawtrey's company, The Private Secretary, *at Manchester, England, but his father, desirous of keeping him off the stage, bribed him to forsake a theatrical career by giving him a half interest in a farm in Harper, Kansas, where he worked for two years.*

Bored with rural life, he again returned to the stage in juvenile roles with Fanny Davenport's company, remaining until the actress' death.

Then came the Alaska gold rush. Taylor traveled to the Klondike and, within nine months, made and lost a fortune.

Over the next few years, he appeared throughout the United States with various stock companies and also made other—albeit unsuccessful—trips to the Alaskan gold fields.

Taylor arrived in Los Angeles around 1912 and, almost immediately, found work as an actor in the then-infant motion picture industry. He was with Thomas H. Ince for nine months and later joined the Vitagraph Company to star in Captain Alvarez.

His first directing job was for the Balboa Company. In 1814, he signed as a director for Famous Players-Lasky where he remained until his death, with the exception of two years, during which he served overseas in the World War as a captain (having risen from the rank of private) with the Canadian Army. Among the stars Taylor directed throughout his career were Mary Pickford, Betty Compson, Mary Miles Minter, Wallace Reid, Dustin Farnum, Constance Talmadge, Jack Pickford, Kathryn Williams, and House Peters. He was about to begin The Ordeal, *a new film with Agnes Ayres.*

William Desmond Taylor, president of the Motion Picture Directors Association, was believed to have been divorced and the father of a daughter in New York City.

I thanked the publicist for the information and told him that the obit would be in the late afternoon edition. However, I'd no sooner hung up than Lundy yelled for me to come to his office.

Actually, Lundy's private office was more like a battered desk and a couple of chairs stuck in the corner of the city room. The *Dispatch*, which was the smallest of the Los Angeles evening newspapers, was housed in a rather primitive structure—a two-story building that had, at one time, been a warehouse. Evidently, when the paper took over, the management, pressed for finances, just set up some simple partitions between departments. Nobody had a private office with four walls.

Lundy was agitated and I really couldn't blame him. His best reporters were at home, sick, and he had a paper to get out.

"Benny," he said, "it looks like that picture director, William Desmond Taylor, has been murdered. I want you to go out on it right away. It could be a big one."

"I just took that over the phone," I replied, somewhat confused. "Ted Taylor at Famous Players called it in. But, he said it was a gastric hemorrhage that killed him."

Andy didn't have time to argue. "I know that. Jerry Grant called from police headquarters. According to his information, when the body was turned over, they found the bullet hole in the back. A squad of cops was just sent over to Taylor's place. So, *get going!*"

Jerry Grant was the *Dispatch*'s police reporter. When something broke down at headquarters, he'd call into the city room and Lundy would dispatch another staff member to follow it up in the field. Today was my turn.

I grabbed my hat and coat, handed the notes Ted Taylor had given me to someone else on the desk (I forget who the hell it was), and told them to write it up—but leave the opening until I phoned in with more details. This was a murder story - a Hollywood murder story - and that kind of copy sold a lot of newspapers.

As I sped (at 25 mph) west on 6th in my trusty Model T, it occurred to me that I'd met Bill Taylor once. It had been at one of those "Hello, pleased to meet you" sort of things at some end-of-production party at Famous Players. My wife, Carol, worked there as a secretary and one night, during the early part of September, 1921, she'd dragged me to this small gathering at which Taylor and several other celebrities were present.

He seemed to be a nice enough fellow - warm and friendly - *very* British. Yet, the one thing that stood out in my mind vividly was how women, beautiful actresses like Claire Windsor and Betty Francisco, fawned over him. I don't think he was without a female at his side all evening. Carol told me later that he had quite a reputation with the ladies.

It took about twenty minutes for me to get from my office to the Alvarado Street address. Taylor lived in a bungalow court located across from Westlake Park, then a fashionable area of Los Angeles. Courts of this type were set on a rather narrow frontage to the street, but ran back quite a distance. The bungalows (in this instance, they were duplexes) were built lengthwise down the lot facing each other, with a landscaped pathway separating them.

The scene was one of mass confusion. Uniformed police, detectives, neighbors in their pajamas, as well as plain, old-fashioned sightseers, were swarming all over the courtyard behaving like nobody knew what was going on or what they were supposed to be doing. It reminded me of something out of a Mack Sennett movie.

Sam "Chubby" Collins, a seasoned photographer from the *Dispatch* staff arrived right behind me. He'd been out on another assignment when Lundy phoned him to meet me at the murder site. We were lucky. It appeared as if we were the first reporters to arrive.

While Sam started on some shots of the house and the court residents, I tried to locate Detective Sgt. Al Drebin, a close buddy of mine and member of the homicide department. Although he was many years my senior, Al and I'd been friends for a long time. When he was a teenager, he'd worked at my father's clothing store and he became almost like a big brother to me. I could always count on him for the "inside" story on any case I was covering. In fact, he was eager to give me the information because he loved to see his name in print (not necessarily as my source, however) and he knew that I'd take care of him on that point.

It looked like the entire homicide squad was out on this one—Cline, Murphy, Winn, Wallace, Cahill, and Cato. Most of them seemed to be just milling around trying to appear busy. Al's shiny bald pate made him easy to spot in the doorway of Taylor's bungalow, talking to Wallace. When he saw me, he grinned, took the unlit stogie from his mouth, and shouted, "Benny, get your shmeckel in here!"

The entry hall and living room were packed with officials. As Al, with his arm around my shoulder, led me to the alcove under the stairs, I caught a glimpse of a sheet covering what was once William Desmond Taylor.

"Ben-a-la," Al said, "have I got a hot one for you. This thing is going to make your rag bigger than the *New York Times*."

"So tell," I said.

"Wait," he protested in his tongue-in-cheek fashion, "let me do my build-up."

"Al, the other papers aren't here yet" I said. "I love you. I love your build-ups. But, give it to me fast."

"You remember how to spell my name?" he said, flicking a piece of lint from my coat.

"Damn it, Al!" I was getting a bit boiled, but I kept my smile and pulled out my notepad.

"Okay," Al said. "Taylor was found when his houseman, Henry Peavey, got to work this morning. Cato is out in the kitchen now, questioning the boy.

"At first, everybody thought Taylor died from natural causes. I can't really blame them. The body was neatly laid out, the limbs stretched out straight, the tie, collar, and the cuffs were unrumpled. The only thing out of place was an overturned chair. Two uniform boys were here, saw nothing mysterious, so they left. A doctor called it a gastric hemorrhage."

"Who discovered otherwise?"

"The assistant coroner and Taylor's boss, some macher from the studio that got called in almost before we were. Eyton's his name. When they started to move the body, there it was - a bullet wound in the left side. He must have been shot at close range because there were powder burns on his coat.

"Now, hear this. The last person known to have seen Taylor alive was Mabel Normand."

That really got my attention. Mabel Normand was one of the biggest stars in pictures. "How much is she involved?"

"Probably not deeply. Evidently, she was having an affair with Taylor. He carried her photo in a locket. But, she was seen leaving with her chauffeur a few minutes before the shot was heard. We've got somebody over at her place now asking questions."

There was a loud commotion outside and we both moved to the door to see what was happening.

Mary Miles Minter, followed by an elderly woman whom I later learned was her grandmother, was making her way through the crowd of police, onlookers and, by this time, other reporters.

Lovely Mary was in her late teens and had succeeded Mary Pickford at Famous Players as the studio's most popular ingénue. According to my wife, she'd also been romantically linked with Taylor.

The girl was weeping hysterically, clawing at her blonde curls as she attempted to gain entrance to the house. Detective Sgt. Hermann Cline met her on the porch and, with the help of her sympathetic grandmother, calmed her down. Quietly, he explained what had taken place and assured her that everything possible would be done to find the guilty party.

Maybe at that point I was forgetting I was a newspaperman, but I really didn't have the heart to start throwing questions at that poor kid. The murder itself was the important story now and, besides, there'd be plenty of time to talk to Mary later. Some of my colleagues, including Sam Collins, weren't as considerate. They followed her back to her car, snapping photos and begging for a statement. (Afterward, Sam told me that Mary denied she was engaged to Taylor, but was extremely sorry she never had been because she admired him greatly as a man.)

Al got busy for a few minutes while the coroner was removing Taylor's body to the Ivy Overholtzer Undertaking Parlor on South Flower Street for autopsy, so I decided to make a quick survey of the house.

The décor of the mulberry carpeted living room was impeccable; a magnificent grand piano, a small mahogany writing desk, and a large tapestry divan being the room's most prominent pieces of furniture. At the desk, Detective Winn was carefully examining an open checkbook, scattered papers, and letters. Several framed, affectionately autographed portraits set on the piano. One caught my eye immediately: "*To my nice Director William Taylor, the most patient man I know. With sincere friendship, Mary Pickford.*"

Mabel Normand had been terser: "*With all the best, always, Bill, Mabel.*"

I pondered a bit over what Miss Minter had written: "*For William Desmond Taylor, artist, gentleman, Man! Sincere good wishes, Mary Miles Minter 1920.*"

Seeing that Al was still occupied, I ventured upstairs. Between the two bedrooms there was a white tiled bathroom with a huge tub.

I don't know what I expected to find in the medicine cabinet, but all that was there were the usual household remedies; a few simple drugs, which indicated that poor Mr. Taylor suffered from such ailments as eye trouble and falling hair. On the other hand, there were perfume bottles with distinctly different odors and other articles pertaining more to feminine tastes than masculine.

The master bedroom, furnished in old ivory, held far more interesting "treasures." In the top bureau drawer, I discovered a filmy nightgown and a variety of ladies undergarments. I was about to turn a pair of these dainties over for a better look at what appeared to be a monogram, when I was interrupted by Sgt. Cahill, who entered the room, followed by Ike St. Johns, Mayor Cryer's press secretary and former reporter with the *Los Angeles Examiner*.

"Birnbaum," glowered the bulldog-faced flatfoot, "what the fuck are you doing in here?" Unlike Al Drebin, Cahill was a cop who felt that reporters should stay "in their place".

"Just soaking up some atmosphere," I smiled.

"Well, soak it up outside. We haven't been through here yet." He pointed to the door, then trailed me downstairs to make sure I didn't double back. Ike stayed in the bedroom.

Al caught my eye just as I was about to be ejected from the house and he ambled over. "Ben-a-la," he said, "have you been getting into things you shouldn't have?"

"Drebin," said Cahill, "just tell your boy to keep his fingers out of the 'cookie jar' or, friend or no, I'll run him in." The good sergeant departed upstairs to rejoin St. Johns.

"Benny," said Al, putting his arm around my shoulder again and leading me to the alcove beneath the stairs, "please don't go exploring on your own. You know I'll take care of you."

"Whatever you say, Al. I promise I'll be good."

Satisfied, my source of information filled me in on the rest of the investigation thus far: Mr. And Mrs. Douglas MacLean—he was the movie comedian and she a former society girl—lived right across the court from Taylor's bungalow. At about 7:30 the previous night, the couple heard the shot that probably killed the director, but assumed it was simply a car backfiring. Faith Cole MacLean had gone to her window and seen a man exiting through the door of the Taylor household. Turning halfway around, the stranger glanced back through the door as if talking to someone there, and then pulled it shut. He spotted Mrs. MacLean and appeared to smile. Without showing any alarm, he then walked away, not to Alvarado Street and the main entrance, but disappeared through the alley leading between Taylor's home and hers. The mysterious visitor was of medium stature, wore dark, rough clothing, and had a muffler and cap on. She could not see his face clearly.

Second, near the back door of Taylor's house, police had found six half-smoked cigarette stubs. This led investigators to speculate that the murderer had waited behind the house until Peavey and Miss Normand departed, then entered through the front door when Taylor left it open while walking the comedienne to her automobile.

Third, although they didn't have all the details on this point as yet, the recently employed Peavey had informed his interrogators that Taylor had sworn out a warrant for the arrest of his former valet—one Edward Sands. It seems that, while the director was in Europe some months back, Sands had allegedly burglarized his home and forged several checks. In fact, Taylor's house had again been broken into twice more during the past few weeks.

Finally, the motive for the slaying did not appear to be robbery, since none of the valuables in the quarters or on Taylor's person were disturbed. Found on the body were about seventy-eight dollars in cash, a two-carat diamond ring, and a platinum watch.

"Look," said Al, as he was being paged to go upstairs, "that's essentially where we are right now. Call that in and check with me later. I'll let you know what's happening."

While we'd been going over the case, Ralph Garson of the *Examiner* had squeezed in behind us to call his story into his paper. Noting this maneuver, Al snatched the receiver out of the burly reporter's hand and bellowed, "For Christ's sake, Garson! Don't you know this phone is for police business only? We're investigating a murder here. Scram!"

Garson gave him a dirty look, then retreated out the front door. Al waited until the newspaperman was out of sight before he handed me the phone. "Be sure you spell my name right," he said as he slapped me on the back. Before I could thank him, he was halfway up the stairs.

I called Andy Lundy directly, told him what I had and that I planned to stay on the story all day. He approved, told me to send Collins back with the photographs for the next edition, and then turned me over to the rewrite desk to dictate my story.

2

It was time to interview the local residents, something that my competitors had been doing for the half-hour I'd been in the house. I collared Collins and sent him back to the paper, then joined the mob of reporters that crowded around the MacLean bungalow.

I was never much of a Douglas MacLean fan. I'd seen him in only one picture—*Captain Kidd, Jr.* with Mary Pickford, which was directed by, of all people, William Desmond Taylor. It wasn't much of a production and, in my view, illustrated that the boyish comic wasn't much of an actor. His brief announcement that neither he nor his wife would answer questions from the press that morning certainly didn't endear himself to me any further.

Other neighbors were more cooperative. E.C. Jessurum, owner of the court, had been ill in bed last night when he heard the shot and called it to the attention of his wife, who was reading to him. Not hearing a second report, they ignored the interruption.

Verne Duma, another court resident, didn't recall if he'd heard the shot or not, but told me that two or three days earlier, he'd observed two men approach Taylor's home, try the door with a key, and then walk away. He didn't know either man, but wondered if one of them could have been the killer.

At the time, Mr. Duma's story didn't strike me as being relevant to the murder investigation. Indeed, there could have been any number of plausible explanations for the men's actions. Perhaps the visitors were workmen who'd been given an incorrect key to the premises, or maybe Taylor had sent some studio personnel to his home to pick something up for him.

The police were keeping Peavey, the houseman, to themselves for the moment, so I decided to take a walk around the neighborhood. Down the way from the Alvarado Terrace Apartments on 6th Street and directly across from Westlake Park—a peaceful two city block expanse of rich green grass, trees and ponds—was the Hartley Service Station. Floyd Hartley, age forty-three, recalled that about six o'clock the previous evening, a dark-haired man in his middle twenties, wearing a blue serge suit and light hat or cap, stopped to ask where "a W.D. Taylor" resided. Since the director was a customer of the establishment, Hartley knew the answer and passed it on to the inquirer, who was last seen heading for the bungalow court.

I walked back to the apartments, trying to retrace the steps the mystery man might have taken several hours before. Passing by the main entrance, I rounded the corner and approached the service alley behind Taylor's apartment. Police were still sifting every foot of the area, seeking an elusive clue they might have missed earlier. Moving up the side of the building, I stopped just short of the court and peered around the corner. It was a perfect vantage point for anyone who'd been waiting here last night to see Taylor and Miss Normand depart the house and walk out to Alvarado Street. Considering the shadows at that time of evening, an assassin could have, within seconds, darted into his victim's quarters undetected.

But, who?

Things seemed to be calming down in the court by now. Many of the curious had departed to go about their business and the other newsmen were either milling around waiting for something to break or trying to talk to one of the court residents into letting them use their phone to call in their information. Some of the more resourceful scribes were doing the same thing I was—trying to uncover fresh story angles.

Detective Captain David Adams had arrived on the scene while I'd been out scouting around. He'd obviously conferred with his men before he stepped out onto the porch to inform the press that he would be holding a five o'clock news conference on the case at police headquarters and, until that time, no further statements would be issued.

The time had come for me to pay Mabel Normand a visit. After all, it was her name in the headlines that was going to sell the papers, not Bill Taylor's. Back in 1922, the public had little, if any, concept of how movies were made. Ask the average moviegoer what a director did and he'd give you a blank stare. But, mention Mabel Normand and their eyes would light up.

Everybody loved Mabel, the beautiful clown, the comic genius who'd starred with both Chaplin and Arbuckle. Next to Mary Pickford, she was the most popular actress in pictures. All one had to do was to look at the box office returns for her films to corroborate the point.

She'd started as a model, posing for such artists as James Montgomery Flagg and Charles Dana Gibson. Her film debut with Maurice Costello at Vitagraph was followed by work with D.W. Griffith. It was through Griffith that the sixteen-year-old actress met an ex-boilermaker named Mack Sennett, who dreamed of making his own movies.

Within a few short years, Sennett had formed Keystone Studios and hired such funny men as Ben Turpin, Ford Sterling, Chaplin, and Arbuckle to star in his one and two reel productions. He also created the Sennett Bathing Beauties and the Keystone Kops. But, his favorite star was none other than Mabel Normand. Mack's madcap ideas had the comedienne leading a lion around on a leash, jumping off cliffs, being run over by cars, thrown from horses and, generally, suffering every other conceivable indignity. Mack gave Mabel the vehicles to become a household name and she, in turn, helped to make him the "King of Comedy."

Everybody knew that the couple loved each other; at least, they did at one time. Mack and Mabel had been engaged for many years. Rumor was that Mack was too busy running his studio (and, possibly, chasing a few girls on the side) to actually take the trip to the altar with Mabel, but two years ago she'd got him to set a date. Then, the day before the wedding, Mabel had called it off, the marriage, the engagement, everything. Nobody really knew why, but gossips were saying that Mabel had stopped by Mack's home one night to find him in the bedroom with actress Mae Bush, her best friend. Nobody could prove it, but that's the story that was going around.

Sennett and Mabel maintained their professional relationship, although, since the split, she'd worked for other producers besides him. As far as William Desmond Taylor was concerned, her name had been linked with his for at least a year now and their pairing appeared, to say the least, an unusual one. She was, if studio publicity releases could be believed, the same screwball off the screen as she was on, whereas his image was that of the suave and sophisticated gentleman.

I must admit that, as a fan, I was rather eager to meet Mabel Normand, despite the unhappy circumstances. She lived in an elegant apartment at Seventh and Vermont, only a mile or so from the Alvarado Terrace Apartments.

My idea to interview her was not unique. I arrived at her residence to find a large grouping of other fourth estate members there ahead of me, including Grace Kingsley of the *Los Angeles Times*. A statement had been promised momentarily and reporters were waiting in the lobby.

I liked Grace Kingsley. She was a striking woman and, like Florabel Muir and Adela Rogers St. Johns (Ike St. Johns wife), possessed a thorough knowledge of this male-dominated profession. All of these women had "paid their dues" and had, thereby, earned the respect of their colleagues.

"It's funny," she offered, as I sat down on a bench next to her.

"What's that, Grace?"

"Mabel hasn't phoned Mack for two years, but the minute she's in trouble, he's the first one she calls."

"How do you know?"

"J.A. Waldron's been in the apartment with her since nine this morning, answering calls and probably coaching her on every word she's going to say to us."

"I can just imagine the sort of response we're going to get from her," I said. "'William Desmond *who*?'"

It was Waldron, Sennett's capable studio manager, who opened the door fifteen minutes later. He explained that, as might be expected, Miss Normand was extremely agitated and would appreciate it if we would keep our questions brief and refrain from taking photographs. Ignoring his pleas, the mob (including Grace and me), kept at bay too long, rushed past the executive and into the fashionable living room.

Mabel, a bit bewildered by the commotion, emerged from her bedroom, attired in a chic green suit, and attempted a smile. She still had that "glow," that inner beauty she radiated from the screen, but make-up couldn't hide her pale features and the fact that she'd been crying. Anticipating our questions, she recited (while flashguns went off around her) a clear and "frank" statement of her movements Wednesday afternoon and evening.

She'd spent most of the day shopping downtown, then at her tax advisor's, and then the bank. When she called home for messages, her maid informed her that Taylor had called to suggest she stop by and pick up a book he'd purchased for her, *Rosmundy* by Ethel M. Dell.

"I arrived at his house about five minutes after seven," she recalled. "We talked about books. I looked around his drawing room and told him I thought he had changed his house furnishings. He said 'You haven't been here for so long you forget.' I hadn't been to his house in two months. He said, 'The Victrola is the only thing new.'

"His servant, Henry, had been arrested for some sort of misconduct, and he was saying that perhaps he would have to go down to court tomorrow (that's today) to see about it. He invited me for dinner, but I told him I had an early studio call this morning.

"Henry left for the night and went out and talked with my chauffeur for a while."

"What's his name?" interrupted Wilson from the *Mirror*.

The question seemed to momentarily knock the comedienne off her prepared train of thought.

Waldman shot the man a nasty look, then answered, "Davis. William Davis. The police have already questioned him."

Mabel continued. "When I left a little while later, Billy walked me to my car and we stood there and chatted for a minute. Then he said he'd call me later, and I drove off.

"I went home, had my dinner, and was in bed and asleep by eight o'clock. I didn't have to go to the studio this morning because there was something the matter with the set."

She hesitated briefly. "Edna Purviance called me this morning and told me the terrible news. I didn't know it was murder until a couple hours later."

I decided to throw her a question, "Did Mr. Taylor have any enemies?"

"I hear that he had told Mrs. Berger (that's Marjorie Berger, who we both use as a tax advisor) he wished that he had called off the warrant he had against Sands. I understand that he felt apprehensive of harm from him. There were, I hear, all sorts of mysterious calls and all that."

"What do you mean by 'mysterious'?"

She didn't, or couldn't, answer that one. Instead she gave me a vacant look that on the screen would have had the audience howling. Here, it merely elicited a few bewildered glances between reporters.

"Mabel," inquired Grace in a woman-to-woman tone, "what was the nature of your relationship with Mr. Taylor?"

The attractive Miss Normand definitely had done her homework for this question. "We have always been great friends. We love to talk over books and that sort of thing. He's the sort of man who can come to the house, sit and read while I play the piano, and talk informally over our work and over our books... at least, he was."

Grace persisted. "Were you engaged?"

The actress smiled sweetly. "Billy had asked me to marry him, but that phase of our friendship has been over for some time. We were just good pals."

The news conference broke a few minutes before three. The only other significant piece of information that came forth was the fact that Henry Peavey's misconduct was an indecent exposure charge. From a news copy standpoint, the thirty minute session had not been disappointing. A couple of intriguing angles, such as Taylor's stated fear of Sands and Peavey's problems, had that bizarre quality city editors relished.

It was perfectly understandable to all of us present as to the reasons why Mabel had seemed less than candid about her relationship with the late director—the future of her new picture, *Molly O*, if not her entire career, was at stake. Aside from any personal feelings he still might hold for the comedienne, Sennett also had a financial interest in her, since together they'd co-produced this recently released production. Any scandal could make its box office potential a dead issue.

Of course, Mack and Mabel weren't the only ones spooked by the Taylor case. Within the next few days, I realized that half of Hollywood was running scared.

When a public figure succumbs, glowing tributes pour in from friends and enemies alike. Indeed, since it isn't always possible to isolate members of the latter group, one of Taylor's eulogies could very well have come from the person who killed him.

The publicity department at Famous Players-Lasky supplied the press with platitudes about William Desmond Taylor from their chief executives.

Jesse L, Lasky, first Vice-President of the corporation, said, *"I have lost a friend, a man who won that place, not only for his personal qualities, but also for the manner in which he discharged his personal duties. William D. Taylor's loyalty to the firm he worked for was proverbial. Never had he been late to any engagement; never had he balked at a task because it was too hard. And when a slump in the industry demanded personal sacrifice, William D. Taylor was the first to offer himself. A man of finer ideals, I have never known.*

"The Famous Players-Lasky Corporation proposes to enter actively into the plans for the detection of the murderer. Resources of time and money will be drawn upon to hasten the time when the murderer of our friend is brought to justice."

General Manager of the studio, Charles Eyton said, *"Through a cowardly assassin's bullet, I have lost the best friend I ever had. I have known Bill Taylor for nine years and we have worked side-by-side for the entire period without an argument or unfriendly word. In all the nine years, I have yet to find a man, woman, or child who was not his friend."*

In San Francisco, Roscoe "Fatty" Arbuckle, awaiting the verdict of his second manslaughter trial, made a statement: *"Mr. Taylor's death comes as a great shock to me. We were good friends and never a whisper of scandal arose about him. He was one of the finest fellows on the lot."*

These and other sentimental remarks awaited me when I returned to the paper at three-thirty to write my follow-up story and make calls prior to the five o'clock news conference.

The early edition was on my desk with the three-inch headline: "FILM DIRECTOR SLAIN, Mabel Normand Questioned by Police." The front page included a large file photo of both Taylor and the actress, a round picture of the bungalow exterior, a shot of Mary Miles Minter's emotional demonstration, and an artist's sketch of the director being shot by a faceless man wearing a cap and muffler.

I was delighted that Lundy had seen fit to give me a byline on the story. He didn't often do this for a reporter, so when he rewarded you in this fashion, it meant "a job well done".

Since Andy was away from his office, I collapsed at my desk, and then suddenly realized that I was famished. I'd been so busy all day that I'd neglected to eat. I called to Jeff, our bespectacled copyboy, who didn't appear to be too busy, gave him half a buck, and told him to run down to the corner snack stand and get me an egg salad sandwich and cream soda.

I wanted to fill in a few blanks, talk to people who knew Taylor pretty well. The best place to find them would be at the studio. Luckily, I had a close relative working at Famous Players who'd be able to steer me in the right direction. I dialed the number and asked to speak to my wife.

Carol and I had met in the spring of 1918, when she'd stopped into my father's Grand Street clothing store to buy a necktie for her brother, Sid, on his birthday. I'd been working in the family business since my Mom died of cancer a few years before. I didn't really enjoy the garment trade (I yearned to be a newspaperman), but Dad hadn't been quite right since my mother's passing and I felt I couldn't desert him.

On that particular afternoon, my father was in the back altering a pair of trousers when the most attractive redhead I've ever seen glided into the store. Her name was Carol Shenson—she was a month younger than me, liked poetry, had a marvelous sense of humor, and was from San Francisco. Her folks had moved there from Philadelphia five months before the 1906 earthquake, but the family was visiting relatives in Los Angeles on that fateful April day.

We took to each other immediately. I asked her to dinner. She accepted. We saw each other constantly during the week she was in town visiting her aunt and uncle. After she returned home, we continued our relationship through the mail and, about every six to eight weeks, either I'd go north for a few days or she'd come down here.

Carol was here when Dad died suddenly from a stroke late the following year. Abraham Birnbaum (1853-1919) had moved to Los Angeles from New York City in 1887. He'd met my mother (the former Sarah Lindberg), who hailed from San Francisco also, pretty much the same way I'd met Carol—she came into the store with her father one day to make a purchase. After their marriage, they worked together side-by-side, with a short time out when I came along, until she died.

It was lonely following my father's death, so I was grateful when Carol decided to move here permanently in order to be closer to me. She lived with her aunt and uncle and got herself a secretarial job at Famous Players, where she'd been ever since.

Having no interest whatsoever in the clothing business, I decided to sell the store and pursue my first love—journalism. I was fortunate. There just happened to be an opening at the *Dispatch* when I applied for work.

Carol and I had been married now for just over a year. We engaged in the usual fights that most young couples go through, but, all in all, I'd say we had a good marriage.

I guess the most common basis for our arguments was that my pride didn't like the fact that she was working. After all, I was supposed to be the bread-winner. I realized, since reporters didn't make the biggest salaries, we could use the extra money, but often my emotions got the best of my reasoning processes. Nevertheless, I knew that, eventually, when she became pregnant (my current project), I'd get my way and she'd have to retire. Ergo, I ultimately let her win the battles, anticipating that victory in the war would be mine.

Her business voice was warm and efficient, "This is Mrs. Birnbaum. May I help you?"

"You certainly can. Who killed William Desmond Taylor?"

"Benny," she sighed, "You don't know what confusion it's been around here today. Are you covering Taylor's death?"

"I've been running around on it all day. What's the gossip at the studio?"

"My God, the executives have been meeting in Mr. Lasky's office most of the day with the door shut. None of them are saying much of anything, but they all seem pretty nervous about the possible repercussions.

"Isn't that terrible about Mabel Normand being involved?"

I glanced at my pocket watch and noted that I really didn't have time to chat with her. "Darling," I said, "I'm up against a deadline right now. Let's go over in detail what happened at the studio at dinner tonight."

She seemed a bit miffed at my cutting her off. "Then why did you call?" she asked.

"Hey, don't get upset. I really want to know what your impression is on this thing, but I've got a news conference at five. We'll go out to dinner and talk about it. Okay?"

That seemed to placate her a bit. "Okay."

"Right now, I was hoping you could switch me over to somebody at the studio who was close to Taylor."

She thought for a minute. "Julia Crawford-Ivers wrote his scenarios for several years. She'd be the best one to talk with."

Carol had my call transferred to Mrs. Crawford-Ivers' office. The obviously distraught woman told me what a "perfect gentleman" her late boss was, and then responded to my question about the mysterious phone calls Mabel Normand had mentioned. "A few weeks before Christmas," she said, "Mr. Taylor told us that he was considerably annoyed and mystified by telephone calls late at night. He said he would answer the phone only to find there was no one at the other end of the wire.

"These calls kept coming at regular intervals, always with the same results. Mr. Taylor said he had not the slightest idea who was calling him or what the purpose was."

"What can you tell me about Taylor's former valet, Sands?" I asked.

"Oh, there was never a more devoted man serving another than this man, Sands, during the first year and a half of his service for Mr. Taylor," the scenarist said. "Mr. Taylor trusted him with everything. Then, he went to Europe and let his English friend, Mr. Edward Knoblock, use his home while he stayed in Mr. Knoblock's house in London. Sands, apparently, had stayed right along in Mr. Taylor's service in Los Angeles and also assisted Mr. Knoblock. Two or three days before Mr. Taylor was to arrive back from London, Sands told Mr. Knoblock that he thought he would take a few days leave of absence but he never showed up again."

"Interesting," I mused.

"Yes, and when Mr. Taylor arrived home from London, he found that Sands had stolen everything, had forged his name to checks, and gone to Hamburgers to buy lingerie (charging it to Mr. Taylor) for his sweetheart. Mr. Taylor didn't even know who she was. Then, there were two more robberies in the house, and Mr. Taylor issued a warrant for the valet's arrest."

"It's hard to believe," I said, "that there were no 'clues' Taylor picked up as to Sands' true character."

"I know," Mrs. Crawford-Ivers said. "He told me Sands read everything he could find. He used to study into the late hours of the night, and when Mr. Taylor talked about the various actions attributed to him, we all decided that the man must have become deranged if he was the one who committed the forgeries."

Jeff returned with my lunch, so I thanked my informant for her cooperation and hung up. It was four thirty. I gulped the meal down in five or six mouthfuls, saw that Andy was back but tied up on the phone, then not wanting to be late, headed for the door and my five o'clock appointment.

Police headquarters was located on the southeast corner of First and Hill in a solid structure built in 1898. The smoke-filled pressroom and its twenty-four hour penny-ante poker game occupied a portion of the second floor.

Jerry Grant had covered the *Dispatch*'s police beat for over eleven years and knew the ins and outs of that department better than anyone. I sometimes thought Jerry actually lived in that pressroom. Every time I saw him, he was wearing the same rumpled suit with a non-matching, loud tie and always seemed to have some sort of snack on his messy desk; a sandwich, cup of soup (when empty, the container was filled with cigarette butts), candy bar, banana, or what-have-you. It could be said that this skinny mid-westerner was L.A.'s version of Chicago's legendary Hildy Johnson.

"Hey, Benny," he called as I entered the nearly empty pressroom. "You did a hell of a job on that story."

"Thanks. Anything break here on it yet?"

"Nobody's been arrested. I was just going down to Adams' office. That's where the rest of the troops are."

We sauntered down the hall to join the other reporters outside the Captain of Detectives office. Garson, of the *Examiner*, was there, as was Grace Kingsley. Adams, an efficient investigator who believed in following Department policy to the letter, didn't keep us waiting.

He began by reviewing the facts that all of us were pretty much aware of: Taylor had been shot, his body "neatly arranged" afterward, Mabel Normand was his last known visitor, the killer probably entered the house while Taylor was walking his guest to her car. Mrs. MacLean had seen a mysterious figure leave the house, and there was a warrant out for Edward Sands on the forgery/burglary charge.

Then, he went into the autopsy report, which he read off his notepad: "A .38 caliber steel-nosed bullet caused Taylor's death. The bullet was found when Autopsy Surgeon Wagner performed the post mortem on the body late this afternoon at the Ivy Overholtzer Undertaking Parlor. The bullet had penetrated the back beneath the left shoulder blade, pierced the heart, and then took a right upward course into the neck, where it lodged. Time of death was between 7:40 p.m. and 8:15 p.m."

Grant popped a question, "A steel-nosed bullet? That's fairly obsolete, isn't it?"

"You don't see too many of them anymore," agreed Adams.

"Captain Adams," I said, "did any of your men speak to the tax advisor, Marjorie Berger, about Taylor's fear of Sands?"

"Oh yes," answered the detective. "He told her just last evening that he had a premonition that something was going to happen to him, but they laughed it off.

"Regarding Sands specifically, Taylor was robbed again in early December of $1,000 worth of jewelry, as well as a large quantity of his specially made cigarettes, which Sands was known to have a yearn for. A week later, a stub from one of those cigarettes was found on Taylor's front doorstep and, according to houseman Peavey, Taylor believed the robber had returned and perhaps been frightened away."

"Surely missing cigarettes doesn't make Sands the guilty party," I prodded.

"I'm getting to that," he snapped. "Later, he got a letter signed 'Alias Jimmy Valentine' in which the writer enclosed pawn tickets for the jewelry. Mr. Taylor recovered the jewelry with these tickets, and when he came to sign a complaint, he explained that the handwriting on the letter—postmarked from Stockton, by the way—was similar to Sands.'"

Garson of the *Examiner* piped up, "Was the man Mrs. MacLean saw Sands?"

"She didn't think so. Mrs. MacLean knew Sands and she didn't note a resemblance between him and the figure she saw. But, of course, we still want to question him on this and the burglaries."

Garson again, "Do you think the man she saw was the killer?"

"That's the theory we're going on at this point. We have testimony from both the streetcar conductor and motorman on the West First Street line, stating that a man wearing a cap and answering the general description of the figure Mrs. MacLean described boarded the car at either 7:54 p.m. or 8:27 p.m. on Maryland Street. That's right behind the bungalow court. They took particular note of him because passengers are rarely picked up at that stop. Unfortunately, neither witness recalls where the man got off.

"Also, a Miss Christine Jewett, the MacLean's maid, remembered hearing somebody running through the service alley behind the bungalows just before the shot was fired.

"Another factor that might interest you," continued Adams, "are reports from Peavey and other court residents that 'mysterious figures' were harassing Taylor and, in one instance, tried to force entry into the bungalow. Taylor, however, chased that prowler away with a pistol. Peavey is not the most reliable witness, but these reports will be checked out."

"Is Peavey under suspicion?" asked Grace.

"At this point, Miss Kingsley, *everybody* is suspect."

"Captain," inquired Jerry Grant, "what are your theories, if any, regarding motive?"

"We're looking into three possibilities right now. First, Taylor had a reputation as a ladies man and it's conceivable that he was shot by a woman he'd scorned. Second, a jealous suitor of one of his lady friends killed him. Or, finally, it was a robbery.

"Now, before you start asking questions, let me say that I'm not prepared to discuss our reasons for theories one or two this evening. We haven't had a chance to delve into these avenues of investigation that deeply yet."

Garson interjected, "I thought robbery was being ruled out because of the money and valuables found on the body."

"That's the one point that works against the third theory," stated Adams. "But, on the other hand, we have the history of multiple robberies in the Taylor household, claims of mysterious prowlers, and the third point is that the bullet holes in Taylor's coat and vest do not match up. One is a few inches higher than the other, as if he had his hands raised over his head when the shot was fired.

"Incidentally, I don't know how much to make of this yet, but we have a report that a man inquired at the Morosco Theater two nights ago for Taylor's residence address and when the doorman told him he didn't know it, the man became very upset."

Adams concluded the interview by informing us that the police administrator was going through Taylor's personal belongings and there would be further information to report on the results of this search later.

Jerry Grant asked, "What kind of liquor supply did he have?"

Adams chuckled, knowing that his answer would infuriate the Prohibitionists. "Good bonded stock hidden in his pantry," he said. "Funny thing though. There was nothing in the liquor cabinet."

The Captain bid us adieu, then went back to work. Jerry and I compared notes for a few minutes, after which we went back to the pressroom to call the story into the rewrite desk.

I was curious about something. Why hadn't Adams mentioned the nightgown and monogrammed feminine undergarments in Taylor's bedroom bureau? Surely the mayor's press secretary, Ike St. Johns, and Sgt. Cahill had discovered them after they'd rousted me.

I located Al Drebin in the men's room taking a leak and put the question to him. "What panties?" he replied with a quizzical look. "We found a nightie and that's it. No monogram."

"Al, don't pull my leg. I saw them. I didn't get a look at the initials, but the panties were monogrammed. That, I'm sure of."

"Benny," said Al, taking the fatherly tone he knew irked me, "you know I level with you. I saw the things myself and there were no panties."

After Al left me to return to his paperwork, I couldn't help but wonder why Ike St. Johns, who was alone in the room while Cahill was escorting me downstairs, would have snatched several pair of pink panties. He certainly was no fairy, so who was he protecting?

I phoned into the paper before I knocked off and spoke to Andy. He'd just finished talking with Jerry Grant and was delighted with the way we were handling the story. Andy was seldom delighted, but since the late edition was going out with an extra-large run, he'd made an exception this time.

Word had just come across the desk that some of the trustees of the Motion Picture Directors Association were considering making an offer of a substantial reward for the arrest of their president's slayer. A meeting was being called that night at the Markham Building in Hollywood, at which time the formal proposal would be presented. Within the next few weeks, Famous Players-Lasky, Mabel Normand and the *Examiner* would make similar gestures.

I told my editor about the disappearing undergarments and he agreed that I should confront Ike St. Johns with my knowledge. I said I'd take care of it on my way to work in the morning because Ike had probably left for the day already and I didn't know where he lived. "Andy," I said before I hung up," something tells me that the truth on this story is going to be hard to come by."

"What makes you think that?"

"The film folk are scared. Not that they're going to lose their lives or suffer physical harm, but their skeletons may be let out of the closets. Look at Ike St. Johns. He's an ex-reporter working for the mayor now, but he still has friends in the picture business and he's protecting them."

"Well, if it's out there, we'll uncover it," soothed Andy. "You've done okay today. Go home. Relax."

It was really a state of panic around the lot today," said Carol, as she sat back in the booth of Mario's Italian Restaurant after the waiter had taken our spaghetti order. We usually came to this intimate little hole-in-the wall when we ate out. The place was clean, a block away from our two-bedroom apartment in Hollywood on Melrose, and, most important, the food was good, served on glass plates, and cheap.

"Mr. Eyton was back and forth to the murder site. He was helping the police with an inventory of Mr. Taylor's personal effects. Mr. Lasky was on the phone with Mr. Zukor several times. Talk is that he's going to come out here."

Adolph Zukor was the New York-based President of Famous Players; Jesse Lasky was First Vice-President, working out of Los Angeles; and Charles Eyton was General Manager of the west coast operation.

I took a sip of water. "The Arbuckle mess all over again, right?"

"Arbuckle... Massachusetts... 'Scandal' was the key word today," Carol said.

"What's Massachusetts?" I asked, not sure I recalled her reference.

She brushed a strand of red hair off her forehead. "Surely, you remember that. 'Fatty' Arbuckle and the Famous Players producers and exhibitors...."

"Of course!" I'd been so busy today, that piece of history had completely eluded my memory.

A few years back in 1917, some Famous Players executives, as well as the roly-poly comic, had been surprised by authorities when their wild orgy, held at Brownie Kennedy's roadhouse outside of Boston, was raided. At the time, a few well-placed pay-offs, allegedly totaling $100,000, had kept the story out of the press. But, some months ago, just prior to the start of the Arbuckle affair, an official of that New England state was indicted for bribery and the entire matter was brought to the public's attention. With the exception of the star, the incident involved mostly east coast names, so the story's impact out here was not as great as it was elsewhere.

Then, in early September of 1921, came the Arbuckle explosion. The star had been hosting a party in his room at San Francisco's St. Francis Hotel. He'd taken Virginia Rappe, a little-known motion picture actress, into his bedroom when guests suddenly heard her agonizing screams coming from behind the closed door. Rushing in, they found Arbuckle standing over the nude girl who was writhing on the bed in pain. Four days later, she died in a hospital of peritonitis, the result of a ruptured bladder.

To avoid sordid newspaper headlines, Arbuckle had returned to Los Angeles, but it wasn't long before he and his attorney were summoned back to the Bay City for questioning. He was subsequently arrested. Rumors were rampant, the most bizarre one being that the comedian had raped the dead girl with the neck of a whiskey bottle.

Following an emotional hearing, a judge ordered Arbuckle bound over to face manslaughter charges, not first degree murder as the prosecutor had wanted.

The funnyman's first trial ended in a hung jury—the vote being 10-2 for acquittal. The second trial had just concluded and a verdict was expected momentarily. Whatever the outcome, Arbuckle was finished in films. We, of the fourth estate in our "saintly" manner of reporting the facts, had seen to that. Our justification: the public had a right to know all about the "immoral fat man" and besides, the story had boosted circulation.

It had been well-sensationalized scandals like these, which had, ultimately, incited reform groups around the country to press for some sort of national censorship. After all, they argued, movies were corrupting the nation's youth. One editorial writer, in fact, suggested a Twentieth Amendment to the Constitution outlawing films the way the Eighteenth prohibited liquor.

To counteract this negative image of the industry, studios would bring reporters out from the eastern papers, wine and dine them, and hope that they'd return home to give the movie industry more favorable publicity. The strategy worked in only some of the cases.

In retrospect, Hollywood of the Roaring '20s was probably saddled with no more sin, bootlegging, drugs, wild parties, or corruption than any other major U.S. city. It simply garnered more attention for its extra-curricular activities because its residents were international celebrities.

Continued press coverage of Arbuckle's problems had acted as fuel for the supporters of national sanctions against the novice film industry. Thus, in January of 1922, the studio bosses had hired incorruptible Postmaster General Will Hays away from President Harding's cabinet to head the newly formed Motion Picture Producers and Distributors Association. Among Hays' duties would be to institute a program of moral self-restraint for films, and thereby try to discourage the threatened censorship proposals. His appointment, a little over two weeks ago, had been widely applauded by the newspapers, but, needless to say, the murder of William Desmond Taylor certainly wasn't going to make his job any easier.

Carol was having a bit of a problem wrapping the spaghetti around her fork. "I'd be surprised if a single roll of film was completely exposed on the lot today," she said. "From what I hear, all everybody did was stand around and speculate about the murder."

"Any interesting theories as to who did it?" I asked.

"How about Mack Sennett?"

Being an admirer of the comedy king, I was surprised at this answer. "How so?"

"I hear that Sennett is a pretty jealous man, especially of anybody Mabel Normand goes out with. He's also been known to be violent at times."

"But," I argued, "it's been over with Mack and Mabel for over two years already."

"That doesn't mean he's not carrying a torch for her."

"Well," I acquiesced, "it might be worth looking into. What else?"

Nothing too much. Somebody thought narcotics might be involved somehow, but they didn't elaborate."

"An interesting idea. See if you can find out more on that angle."

Carol chuckled. "Benny, you're beginning to sound like your editor."

We continued to enjoy our meal and each other's company, staying at the restaurant until nine thirty. As we strolled home, arm-in-arm, I verbalized a thought that had occurred to me at dinner: "It's an enigma," I said.

"What is?"

"The picture industry. It's a multi-million dollar business, but the industry's principal assets are these personalities."

"What do you mean?" Carol asked.

"Look at them: Sennett is an ex-boilermaker; Mabel Normand was a factory girl before she started modeling; some of the stars are former truck drivers or waitresses; and I'm sure there's a female star or two who, at one time, was a prostitute. Now, all of a sudden, these people, who yesterday had to scratch for a living, are residing in mansions, earning thousands of dollars per week, and a lot of them don't really know how to handle this newly found wealth and social status. So, they get into trouble. It's like putting a four-year-old in a toy shop and telling him to play.

"But, without these former members of the laboring class, the movies wouldn't draw in half the revenue they do."

Carol seemed a bit concerned. "I suppose you're right," she muttered.

"What's the matter?"

"Oh, nothing really. It's just that when you mentioned prostitution, it reminded me of some of the young girls I see in the casting office."

"In what way."

"Some of them look like they haven't had a decent meal in days. Yesterday, I had to deliver some forms there. The receptionist had a box of cookies on the desk. One girl, her face was so gaunt, came out of the casting director's office. She obviously didn't get hired. She saw the cookies, and when she thought nobody was looking, grabbed a handful and ran out.

"It's just sad to see these lost girls come to town with such high hopes of getting into pictures. Most of them get nowhere and, when they run out of money, a lot of them must become prostitutes. What else is there for them? It's depressing."

I had to agree with her. "Any time you've got an industry built on dreams and make-believe, the reality of it has got to be depressing."

Ike St. Johns wasn't in his office when I stopped by on Friday morning. His secretary informed me that he was in a conference with the mayor and that he would be unavailable most of the day. I left my card, asked that she have her boss phone me, and then departed for police headquarters.

I found Al Drebin in his office, sipping coffee and going over some reports. He seemed surprised to see me. "Benny," he said, "I thought you'd be at the paper by now. I just sent a witness over to see you. You'll want to interview him."

"Who is he?"

"Let him tell you."

He pulled some notes from the mess on his desk. "Got a couple more items that might interest you," he said. "Chief of Police in Fresno found some of Taylor's jewelry pawned in Sacramento."

"Sands?" I asked, scribbling on my note pad.

"Looks that way. Then, we have an account from a Mrs. Ida Garrow, who lives in the Rose of Sharon Apartments. She was walking near Taylor's bungalow about eight thirty Wednesday night. A suspicious looking man was ahead of her, and when a police officer appeared walking down the block toward them, the man scurried across the street and disappeared into the shadows."

"Eight thirty... that's not long after the murder."

"She described the figure as being short and heavy-set. That's Sands' general build."

"Is the department going to formally accuse him?"

"We don't know yet. But, there's another item." He referred to a sheet of paper with typing on it. "This is a statement from a Mr. A.A, Tomlinson. He contacted us early this morning after he read the *Examiner*… So, why doesn't he read the *Dispatch*?"

"No idea," I shot back. "What did he say?"

Al read what the accountant, who lived on West 40th Place, had to relate:

"*The true name of this man is not Sands, but Strathmore. I recognized him by his picture in this morning's* Examiner. *He enlisted in the Army during the war as Edward Fitz Strathmore and was assigned to Columbus Barracks, Ohio. I was then head of the finance office, and upon hearing that Strathmore had been a Chief Petty Officer in the Navy, I asked that he be transferred to my department, which was done.*

"*On October 4, 1919, Strathmore forged my name to a government check for $475 and tried to buy a motorcycle with it. He failed to carry out his scheme, but escaped. At the same time, he forged the commanding officer's name to a discharge. He had been wanted for desertion.*

"*On July 4, 1920, I met him on Alvarado Street. He told me he was expecting to get work with the streetcar company. I notified the police, but he disappeared. During his service with me at Columbus Barracks, Strathmore often boasted of the crimes he had committed. I did not believe him then, but I thought it was a case of a young fellow drawing on his imagination. Once I asked him what he would do if he were in a dangerous situation. He said he would shoot his way out.*

"*Strathmore gave me a number of books, all bearing his signature on the inside of the cover. In each case, Strathmore had written over a name which had been erased. In one of those, I was able to make out the erased name of 'Sands.'*"

"We wired the Columbus Barracks for a description of Strathmore, and we just received the answer," Al said, referring to a telegram. "'*Dark complexion, ruddy-faced, height 5'6," slightly bowlegged.*' It's Sands.

"Oh, yes," he continued, "I nearly forgot… you can have fun with this one, but for obvious reasons, the guilty party shall remain nameless."

"One of the boys in blue screw up?" I asked.

Al nodded. "That's right. Late last night, this 'super-sleuth'— he was one of the first cops into Taylor's living room—recalled that there'd been a soiled handkerchief a few feet away from the cadaver. He didn't think it was anything, so he just laid it on a coffee table and when he remembered it awhile later…."

"It was gone," I interrupted.

"Right! But, according to what this gumshoe says, there was an initial on the thing."

"'S,'" I submitted.

"'S.' Could have slipped out of the killer's pocket."

Al's phone rang—the caller apparently summoning him elsewhere.

"Look, Benny," he said, getting "fatherly" again as he walked me to the hallway, "this Sands angle looks pretty good right now, but don't put all your eggs in that basket. There's a lot here we're working on that I can't tell you yet and the direction of the investigation could change any minute."

"You've got something on the jealously motive?"

Al nodded.

"What if I promised that I wouldn't use it?"

"Then why know?"

"Curiosity."

Al loved to confide secrets to me—like a kid wanting to tell his brothers and sisters what they were getting for Christmas. He felt safe letting me on in these suppressed developments because I never printed anything he asked me not to.

"Just between us on this one thing?" he said.

I nodded to give him the assurance he didn't need.

"We found two strands of blonde hair on Taylor's lapel."

He stopped me before I could present the obvious question.

"We don't know who the woman is or even if she was there when the murder was committed. He could have had them on his person for hours, if not days, before he was shot. And with that, I leave you."

He walked across the hall and entered Captain Adams' office before I had the chance to ask the half dozen questions that were spinning in my head. Al could always make the most dramatic exit when he wanted to.

Theodore Kosloff was an actor/dancer and, at least on the surface, fit my preconceived idea of what all male dancers should look like—slender with delicate features. He was waiting for me in the sitting room when I arrived that morning. After informing me in his best theatrical tones that Drebin had sent him, I invited him to sit next to my desk and relate his information.

Some weeks ago, the performer had been working in a picture, *The Green Temptation*, directed by William Desmond Taylor. "We were on location," he stated, "a place in the country, and were walking together, chatting. Suddenly, from behind a clump of brush, a man arose, almost with a spring." Kosloff, indeed, sprang from his chair.

"Quicker than the surprising stranger was Taylor. He leaped around to one side to face the man," as did my dancer "friend"—a move that attracted the attention of everyone in the city room.

"They stood eye-to-eye for a moment, neither speaking. Then the man turned and walked away."

Kosloff stood silent. After a few seconds, I ventured, "And, then?"

"That's all. Mr. Taylor and I went on with our conversation."

"He didn't explain the incident?"

"I didn't think it was my business, so I didn't ask."

"I see,"

I did see. My old buddy, Al, was having a little fun by sending over one of his "screwballs." I motioned my visitor to the exit. "I want to thank you for coming in, Mr. Kosloff, and sharing this with me."

"Is my name going to be in the paper?" he asked.

"Probably."

"Wonderful! The name's spelled K-O-S-L-O-F-F."

"I have it. Thank you again." Perturbed, I watched the publicity seeker depart, and then looked at the faces of my colleagues. They were laughing and I couldn't help but join them. I did a poor imitation of Kosloff's movement, and went over to Andy's office.

"The coroner's inquest is tomorrow," said the editor, as I sat down and pulled out my notepad. "You going to be there?"

"You know me better than that."

Tomorrow was Saturday, the Sabbath. Lundy was well aware that I wouldn't work that day, although on this story I was tempted. But, he had to make a token gesture.

"Okay," he said. "Absenteeism has diminished today. I'll have Sandy Haines cover it. What else is new?"

I filled him in on what I'd learned from Carol last night, as well as from Al this morning, omitting the part about the blonde hairs. It was my plan to go back to Alvarado Street to see if I could talk to some of the neighbors I'd missed yesterday. The jealousy angle called for further probing, as did Carol's references to narcotics.

"By the way," Andy said, "be sure to use what your athletic friend gave you. It'll add color."

I chuckled at his reference to Kosloff and returned to my desk.

Additional tributes to the deceased had come in over the wire since yesterday. From New York, Cecil B. DeMille, debarking from the *Aquitania* after his return from Europe, said of Taylor: "*There was not a cleaner man in the motion picture industry. He was never engaged in any questionable relations with women of his acquaintance.*"

More interesting had been the account wired in from Phoenix, Arizona. A "Frenchy" Ed Raymond recalled working with Taylor and writer Jack London in the late 1890s amid the Alaskan Gold Rush: "*Taylor was a strong man with a strong man's vices. His one passion was gambling, at that time not regarded as a fault among the bold men who searched for gold. It was the only pastime they had at their command.*

"*And even at his one lone deviation from the paths of righteousness, he was a leader and commanded respect and admiration from all who knew him. He was a plunger of the squarest type, but was withal a quiet, reserved gentleman who never in my memory was seen in controversy.*"

According to Raymond, he first met Taylor in Dawson in 1899, and knew him until the summer of 1900. At that time, Taylor was working a profitable lease near Dawson. Raymond left Alaska in 1900, and only heard of Taylor through mutual acquaintances until the report of the murder.

I began to write my updated and recapped story for the early edition, figuring that I'd utilize these recollections as background material. My account emphasized the strong evidence that was building against Sands, but left an escape should the wind change. The jealousy and narcotics angles were mentioned in passing.

The story complete, I turned it over to the desk and was going out the door on my way to the Alvarado Terrace Apartments when the phone rang. The caller introduced herself as Mrs. Ada Deane-Tanner.

"I can tell you all about William Desmond Taylor," she said. "I'm his sister-in-law."

It took "Chubby" Collins and me about an hour to drive the eighteen miles from the Los Angeles City Center to Monrovia, a small town just east of Pasadena. Ada Deane-Tanner lived in a modest yellow-frame house at the very rural 426 Lemon Avenue.

The woman had been quite explicit when she'd phoned. As the sister-in-law of William Desmond Taylor, she claimed to have in her possession some shocking new facts about the dead man, which would, supposedly, change the entire complexion of the investigation. Andy and I agreed that she sounded legitimate and that I should make the trek out to the "sticks." I briefed Sandy Haines, a promising young cub reporter about three years my junior, and he went back to Alvarado in my place.

I understood, or at least assumed, from Mrs. Deane-Tanner that the *Dispatch* would be getting an exclusive interview. Yet, to my surprise and consternation, upon our arrival at her home, I found both Garson of the *Examiner* and Grace Kingsley of the *Times*, as well as their respective photographers, waiting on the porch to be admitted.

"She really called everybody, didn't she," I commented as I walked through the gate.

Grace chuckled, but Garson, as was his custom, simply gave me the cold shoulder. Garson and I didn't like each other and hadn't for most of the two years since we'd met. Aside from the fact that I didn't approve of the *overly* sensationalized yellow journalistic technique both he and his editor practiced, Garson was an anti-Semite.

Shortly after I'd met the reporter, Andy Lundy and I were in a speakeasy enjoying a beer. Garson, obviously in a bad mood, wandered in, had three shots in short order, and then proceeded to make some anti-Semitic remarks. That's one area where I have no tolerance. Without hesitation, I picked up my half-empty beer pitcher and cold-cocked him. I don't think we'd exchanged ten words since. Big loss!

"Did Sennett send somebody to coach her, too?" I asked Grace, referring to the fact that we were, like yesterday, being asked to wait outside until our hostess was ready to see us.

"The cops are questioning her right now," she said. "We don't get in until they leave."

"That's just great," complained Chubby. "I've got other things besides this to shoot this afternoon."

We were lucky. Detective Sergeants Cato and Cahill finished their interrogation within twenty minutes. Cato beckoned us into the house as he departed with, "You people better tell your editors to hold the front page for this one."

Mrs. Deane-Tanner was a rather emaciated woman in her mid-forties. She might have once been considered attractive, but that beauty was faded now, the result of too many years of illness, disappointment, and despair.

She seated us in her meagerly furnished living room, and then when she was sure she had our complete attention, began her strange tale which, without a doubt, made our trip to Monrovia well worth the time and trouble. She told it not without prejudice, being quite bitter about the way life and the Deane-Tanner brothers had treated her.

It seems that William Desmond Taylor was *not* William Desmond Taylor at after all. Nor had he been the pillar of virtue, as claimed by his friends. His real name was, in fact, William Cunningham Deane-Tanner. Born in Dublin into a wealthy family, he came to the United States in his late teens and went to Runnymede, a settlement near Harper, Kansas, established by Ned Turnley in 1887 for remittance men, the impoverished sons of English nobility.

Sporting a mustache, he eventually moved to New York City where, in 1901, he met and married Miss Ethel May Harrison, a member of the original Florodora Girls. She bore him a daughter.

Deane-Tanner/Taylor, at that time, was vice-president of the English Antique Shop, owned by a Mr. A.J. Crawford and located on Fifth Avenue between 27ᵗʰ and 28ᵗʰ. With an estimated annual income of $25,000, he was very active in the affairs of the Larchmont Yacht Club.

Ethel had been well educated by her once well-to-do broker father and was a pianist of some ability. Her uncle was multi-millionaire realtor/importer Daniel J. Braker. During his marriage to Ethel, Deane-Tanner borrowed a considerable amount of money from Braker and wasted it on extravagances. He had a reputation as a heavy drinker and a womanizer. When the uncle died in 1908, the future film director expected to be remembered handsomely in the will, yet the deceased's actual gift to the young "fortune hunter" was quite a disappointment: "*To W.C.D. Tanner, I leave and bequeath the amounts of money owing to me by him.*"

About a week after the will was probated, Deane-Tanner attended the Vanderbilt Cup Race on Long Island with a group of friends. Two days later, he sent a note to an assistant at the antique shop, instructing that he should bring him $600 cash at the Broadway Central Hotel. The assistant found his employer there, sans mustache and seemingly quite agitated. Deane-Tanner kept $100 of the money, told the young man to deliver the remainder to his wife, then dismissed him.

That was the last anybody ever saw of William Cunningham Deane-Tanner. The date was October 26, 1908.

At first, the family could assign no reason for the man's disappearance except aphasia. In 1912, Mrs. Deane-Tanner got a decree of divorce in the state of New York and was awarded custody of the couple's only child, Ethel Daisy, then nine years old. Two years later, she married Edward L.C. Robins, owner of a number of Manhattan restaurants, including Delmonico's.

Is it any wonder why William Desmond Taylor's official studio biography failed to mention this episode in his life?

William Deane-Tanner bore a strong resemblance to his younger brother, Dennis, who served with the British Army as a lieutenant during the Boer War. The younger Deane-Tanner arrived in New York sometime after his sibling, obtained a position as manager of a rival antique shop on East 45ᵗʰ Street and, in 1907, married Miss Ada

Brennan (our hostess). Dennis was looked upon as the counterpart in courtesy and culture of his brother. But, also like William, he had a fondness for the company of women other than his wife.

Two years after William's disappearance, Dennis Deane-Tanner vanished also, leaving a wife, ill with tuberculosis, and two small children. Ada came back from the sanitarium in the Adirondacks, where she'd been recovering from her disease, and with the help of the police conducted a long and unsuccessful search for her husband. Eventually, she moved to Monrovia, where she had relatives.

In 1914, Ada had gone to the movies to see *Captain Alvarez*. There on the screen in the starring role was her brother-in-law, William Deane-Tanner, acting under the pseudonym of William Desmond Taylor.

Immediately, the enlightened woman dispatched a letter containing news of her find to her former sister-in-law, Ethel, who had recently married Mr. Robins. The ex-Mrs. Deane-Tanner was not too surprised, since she'd already discovered on her own that William had become a movie actor.

After some investigation, Ada located the residence of William Desmond Taylor in Hollywood and confronted him. The then-actor denied her accusation, claiming she was suffering from a case of mistaken identity. Yet, when she became ill again, Taylor sent her a monthly allowance of $50 and continued payments until the present.

"Perhaps he was afraid of what the scandal would do to his career if I went to the press," suggested Mrs. Ada Deane-Tanner. "Not that I ever intended to. I just wanted him to tell me where my husband was."

"Have you ever discovered the whereabouts of Dennis?" inquired Grace.

Ada shook her head.

"What about Taylor's daughter?" I asked. "Has she been in contact with her father?"

"I think they wrote to each other, but I'm not sure. As I said, Mr. Taylor never actually admitted to me he *was* Dennis' brother."

Chubby and I had a good laugh as we drove away from Ada Deane-Tanner's home in search of a telephone so I could call the paper. William Desmond Taylor, Hollywood's man of "impeccable" reputation, had fallen from grace. Not only was he a heavy drinker and a womanizer, but he also deserted his wife and young daughter. The public was going to love reading about this.

I gave the story to Andy, who decided it warranted putting out an "extra." Haines wasn't back from Alvarado Street yet, but Lundy related one new development in the case.

County Sheriff William I. Traeger had assigned two of his best deputies to work with the police department on the investigation. Of course, the law enforcement official already had his own theory as to the crime's solution, which Andy read to me: "*It is my present belief that some woman who mistook Taylor's natural courtesy and genuine kindness and sympathy as evidence of affection, and whom he was compelled to disillusion, induced some man, possibly already unfriendly to the director, to watch his house, perhaps for several weeks, to familiarize himself with the dead man's habits. Having become acquainted with Mr. Taylor's movements, it then was but a question of waiting for the opportune time.*"

The statement went on to explain how the killer must have entered the house while Taylor was walking Mabel Normand to her car and shot him dead upon his return.

"*When there was no alarm from the sound of the shot, the slayer apparently calmly pocketed his revolver, stepped out of the house, and could easily have escaped in a waiting automobile or out the window into the alley, which parallels the house from there to the street, without attracting undue attention.*"

"Well," I mused, "that'll be great fodder for Traeger next time he's up for re-election… assuming he's correct in his theory."

Andy laughed. "Oh, he's covered his rear. He, naturally, starts out by saying that this hypothesis is based on the *limited* facts now in his possession."

"Figures. What else is new?"

"The Arbuckle jury deadlocked again. Third trial is set to start March 13."

"That'll sell a few more papers."

"By the way," interjected Andy, "you know where Mary Miles Minter went after she left Taylor's apartment yesterday? Right over to the funeral parlor. She wanted to view the cadaver, but they wouldn't let her."

"That doesn't surprise me. She wasn't in the best of shape."

I told the editor that I'd drop Chubby off at the paper, and then I was going to stop by police headquarters before I came in to write my updated story. It was nearly two o'clock, and I knew that sundown tonight would be about six. I had to be finished at work and home by then so that Carol and I could walk to *shul*.

Al Drebin was driving out of the police parking lot when I arrived at headquarters. Even when he was in a hurry, my mentor always had time to stop and spend a minute or two with me. Taking the unlit stogie from his mouth, he asked, "So, Ben-a-la, how was Monrovia?"

"Unbelievable. How did you guys get onto it so fast?"

"Excellent police work. Besides, the Captain got a call from Mrs. Deane-Tanner this morning about the same time you were in my office."

"Do you think the killer's somebody from that area of Taylor's past?

"How the hell should I know?"

"Don't get upset, *schmuck*," I said. "I gotta ask the questions. That's why they pay me all that money."

"I'll tell you one thing," offered Al.

"Please do."

"You know the valuables supposedly stolen by Sands that were recovered from Fresno and Sacramento?"

"What about them?"

"Some of the items were pawned in the name of 'William Deane-Tanner,' and the tickets mailed back to Taylor. You figure it out." He put his car into gear.

"Wait a minute," I protested.

"Can't. Doran of the D.A.'s office is over at the County Supervisors right now waiting for me. Wants help in preparing a diagram of Taylor's house and the immediate surroundings. Love ya.'"

He pulled out of the driveway and turned down Hill, leaving me standing there with my mouth slightly agape. Evidently, Sands, or whoever had robbed Taylor, knew all about his past life.

In the pressroom, the perennial poker game was in session, but Jerry Grant was at his desk reading the just-delivered "extra" edition of the *Dispatch*. Headline: TALOR'S SECRET PAST REVEALED. Again, I had my byline.

The police reporter complimented me on my scoop—we'd beaten the other papers to the street by at least an hour—then he invited me to walk around the block with him. Jerry needed to get out of that miserable gray-walled building a couple times a day, and some fresh air, no matter what the outside temperature, was the perfect prescription to clear his head.

It was a little chilly as we came out of the structure and headed south on First. Jerry echoed my surprise when I told him about the pawn tickets bearing the Dean-Tanner moniker, but could offer no plausible explanation for the thief's behavior.

"There's not a hell of a lot happening here today," he reported. "You got the big one in Monrovia."

"No statements from Adams?"

"He thinks the killing was too well planned to be the work of an amateur, and that the culprit was definitely the man Mrs. MacLean saw.

"They're questioning a lot of witnesses. Harry Fellows, Taylor's assistant director, was here for a couple of hours. The thinking is that he was close enough to Taylor to be able to give them a pretty good idea as to what his movements were during the last few days.

"Then, there's talk that some of the bulls are out interviewing Taylor's actress friends - Claire Windsor, Betty Francisco.... All of them claim complete ignorance of his private life. Oh, yes, right now, they're chatting with Mr. And Mrs. Earl Tiffany. He was Taylor's chauffer before Howard Fellows, Harry's brother, got the job."

"Why did he quit?" I asked, as we rounded the corner of Broadway and Second.

"He was fired. Seems he kept a written record of every place he took our late friend and Taylor didn't appreciate that."

"I'd love to see that record."

"Wouldn't everybody?"

Grant mentioned one other point the authorities were investigating. Two different witnesses near Alvarado and Maryland had seen two "mysterious" automobiles on the night of the murder, about the time the Normand vehicle arrived at the bungalow court. One informant described one car as a large, open, high-priced motor coach painted chocolate brown, while the other witness had said it was green and closed. Police weren't really sure if either car had anything to do with the case, but they were checking them out nevertheless.

I bid Jerry goodbye on the steps of the police building and he promised to call me after the interrogators were finished talking to the Tiffanys.

When I got back to the *Dispatch*, Sandy Haines was at his desk, typing the results of his day's investigation. He'd done an admirable job. Aside from securing information about the two "mysterious" cars from Sgt. Herman Cline, who he'd interviewed at the murder site, the cub reporter had also spoken to the Douglas MacLean's butler, Carl.

Carl didn't have a very high opinion of Edward Sands. He described the missing valet as being a "shifty-eyed individual" who lacked the cultivated subservience necessary for his position. On one occasion, the butler had asked him where he had previously been employed and Sands had snapped back, "None of your business."

The servant also told Hines that, according to Peavey, Mabel Normand had recently given Taylor a black amber cigarette holder worth $1,800 and that he'd presented her with a $1,200 dress.

I wished I could afford to buy Carol a $1,200 dress, or even a $100 dress.

I was composing my final story of the day, rushing to get out of the office by five fifteen, when Jerry Grant called in with his promised report of the Earl Tiffany interrogation.

The former chauffeur claimed that, in December of 1920, he'd driven Taylor to Los Angeles' Chinatown for the purpose of attending a "hop" or opium party, for which that district was famous. The director told his employee he did not intend to partake in this "forbidden delight," but he wanted to view the scene as research for an upcoming film. Whether Taylor had actually smoked this derivation of the poppy, Tiffany didn't know. However, he was aware that other Hollywood personalities often visited these dens.

"Did he name the personalities?" I asked.

"No. I think that aspect was just hearsay on his part."

"What did he have to say about Sands?"

"Young man," chuckled Jerry, "I thought you'd never ask."

Like most of us in the newspaper game, as well as my buddy, Sgt. Drebin, Jerry enjoyed building up the suspense whenever he had a piece of "hot" news to relate.

"Are you ready for this?" he continued. "Tiffany knew Sands rather well. In fact, Sands had visited the Tiffany home more than once."

"When did they last see him?"

"Mrs. Tiffany saw Sands on January 31st, the day before the murder, standing in the doorway of a shop near Sixth and Figueroa."

"Was she sure? I thought he'd skipped town."

"He did quit the city. But, that's not all. He said something to her."

"What?"

"'I came back to get that son-of-a-bitch Taylor.'"

7

I didn't pay much attention to what went on in the synagogue that Friday night. I'd been completely hooked by the William Desmond Taylor murder, and Jerry Grant's late afternoon call about Mrs. Tiffany having heard Edward Sands threaten his former employer was the thing that finally got me.

It's difficult to say what it was about this mystery that intrigued me beyond my normal journalistic curiosity. Certainly I was no avid fan of detective fiction, so I wasn't out to do a Sherlock Holmes number. Perhaps I was getting annoyed that the case was becoming a bit too easy; that the solution was being handed to us (the police and the press), almost as if a novelist was creating new evidence daily in his overly coincidental "who-done-it."

The case against the missing Edward Sands was approaching monumental proportions. He'd allegedly stolen from his employer, as well as others during his lifetime; he may have known about Taylor's secret past; *possibly* he was seen in the area the night of the murder; and, the day before that, a seemingly disinterested witness heard him threaten Taylor. Then, one couldn't forget the elusive handkerchief bearing the initial "S." The evidence was definitely circumstantial; but, on a good day, the district attorney could get a conviction on it.

And yet, something was missing… *the motive.*

Why should Sands kill Taylor? Because the director had sworn out a warrant for his arrest? That didn't seem likely.

Maybe Sands tried to rob Taylor and, in the attempt, killed him. But, if that were true, why didn't he take the valuables off the corpse?

They were worth close to $2,000. Ergo, robbery was not the probable motive.

On the other hand, perhaps Sands was plain crazy and killed Taylor for his own twisted reasons. That was possible, but at this point, it seemed too much of a long shot to reasonably consider.

I felt it was time the police looked a bit more closely at some of the other material items that had, temporarily, been placed on a back burner while the Sands theory was being pursued. For example, the mysterious stranger seen around Taylor's home; the blonde hairs found on his body; the nightgown and ladies under things in the bureau (I still had to confront Ike St. Johns on that matter); the deceased's interest in numerous women; and, his explorations into the opium dens of Chinatown.

Sands could very well be the culprit, but these other avenues should be investigated also. Just because the valet currently appeared to be the easiest answer to the puzzle, didn't mean he was the correct one.

I'd been depending on Carol to give me some insight into what was going on behind the well-guarded walls of Famous Players, but her report proved to be a disappointment. She'd hardly been in the studio at all Friday. Upon her arrival at work, she'd been sent out to take care of some insignificant errands that were to keep her off the lot for the entire day.

Funny, her duties as a secretary had never taken her away from the studio for that length of time before. Perhaps it was just a coincidence that this change of routine was happening now, or maybe somebody didn't want certain information to reach the eyes and ears of the wife of a newspaperman who was covering the Taylor case.

Or, maybe I was a bit paranoid.

I was up half the night mulling over the facts of the murder and, the next day, it was all I could do to keep from picking up the receiver and calling into the paper to see what was going on. Indeed, about noon, the phone did ring for about five minutes, and I knew it had to be Andy Lundy trying to reach me, making a vain attempt to coerce me into going out on an assignment. But, I'd practiced my religion far too long to submit to the temptation of answering Mr. Bell's invention.

Aside from wanting to know how the investigation was progressing, I longed to attend the coroner's inquest. Sandy Haines did and, when I phoned the paper after six o'clock, he described to me the events that transpired.

The hearing was conducted by Coroner Nance at the Ivy Overholtzer undertaking parlor—in a somber room next to where the murdered director's body lay covered with a satin pall. The jury was seated at a long wooden table with a straight-backed witness chair placed beside it. A large crowd, obviously gathered to hear film stars testify, must have been disappointed, as Mabel Normand was the only prominent actress who appeared on the stand. The comedienne was herself fifteen minutes late, sneaking in through the rear of the establishment to avoid reporters and photographers. Also in attendance were Mr. And Mrs. Douglas MacLean and Edna Perviance, however they were not called to testify.

Charles Eyton, the very proper western manager of Famous Players-Lasky was the first witness. He grimly told of finding the body and how he and Mr. MacLean had supposed death was due to natural causes until the assistant coroner ordered the body removed and the bullet wound was discovered. Then, after autopsy surgeon Wagner described in his matter-of-fact fashion the path of the bullet, Miss Normand was called.

Dressed in a fashionable brown checked sport coat furred at the collar and cuffs, a black skirt, and a wide-brimmed green fedora atop her head, the actress took the stand. Her voice was low, as she recalled to the jury the events that took place on the evening of February 1st.

"Did Mr. Taylor go with you to your car when he left?" was the question.

"Yes, he took me to the car and stood talking with me a few minutes and said he would call me by telephone in about an hour. He watched while I drove away and I waved my hand to him."

"Did he call you up?"

"No. I went home and went right to bed. My maid never wakes me anyway, once I have retired."

It was Henry Peavey's turn next. The effeminate Negro had been Taylor's houseman for about six months and he'd been in the bungalow when Mabel arrived.

Strange, but Peavey was the only person to display any type of emotion throughout the entire proceeding. Upon his arrival at the undertaking parlor, he'd knelt on the floor by the bier and sobbed aloud. Later, his wails were frequent during his entire testimony.

"I saw them (Taylor and Mabel) setting on two chairs facing each other in the living room," he said. "They were talking about a red-covered book they were handling. I went out after locking the back door. The front door has a spring lock. I talked to Miss Normand's chauffeur a minute, then went on."

Peavey proceeded to tell how he discovered Taylor's body the next morning and, again he broke down, unable to continue for some time. His mourning sounded so much like a guffaw that it brought smiles to the lips of many spectators.

Tears in his eyes, Peavey continued, "I went out and yelled that Mr. Taylor was dead."

"Had anything been changed?"

"Nothing, except that the chair was overturned. The lights were on and the back door was locked. Nothing was taken that I know of."

Lieutenant Tom Ziegler, who'd been one of the first detectives on the murder scene, was the final witness. Testifying before Coroner Nance and his jury had become a habit after so many years of homicide investigation. The essence of his statement was that suicide in this instance was a total impossibility.

The coroner ordered the room cleared of spectators while the jury deliberated and, this done, it was only a matter of minutes before the verdict was reached: "that Taylor had come to his death at the hands of an assassin."

So, what else is new?

What *was* new on Saturday was that things were beginning to "pop" on the case in a variety of directions. It was rumored that Sands, being sought at this point as a material witness in the investigation, had been found, questioned, and placed in secret custody. However, a little digging by the *Dispatch* staff proved that the story was without foundation.

More data was dispatched by the police regarding the .38 slug that killed Taylor. The fact that it was a steel-nosed bullet of a type that had not been manufactured for years and is not found on sale in an up-to-date store led police to conclude that the assassin did not recently buy the revolver or ammunition, but had both in his (or her?) possession for a number of years. Nevertheless, the Department was beginning a systematic search of all stores dealing with firearms to secure facts regarding recent purchases.

The police were also, thankfully, looking into areas beyond the Sands theory. Spurred by reports from ex-chauffeur Earl Tiffany that Taylor had visited opium dens in Chinatown, detectives began running down known Los Angeles drug dealers to see if they could add further clues that would help unmask the killer. Since it had long been rumored that several of filmdom's most prominent personalities were addicted to some type of drugs, knowing who these people were could be the key to unlocking the puzzle.

The authorities were starting to interview a number of Hollywood folk who had supposedly known Taylor well. Young Mary Miles Minter, endowed with blonde curls, was one of the first to be questioned at her home, where she was reported to be ill, by Captain Adams.

Though encumbered with an antagonistic "stage" mother, who was disliked and shunned by most of the motion picture community, sweet Mary had become one of Famous Players' most valuable stars, having taken over the innocent ingénue assignments Mary Pickford abandoned when she'd broken from the studio some years before. Several of Miss Minter's films on the lot, including *Anne of Green Gables*, her most successful, which had been directed by William Desmond Taylor and it was, therefore, understandable that she would be quite upset over his death. However, in retrospect, one would have to ponder if her totally hysterical reaction at both the murder site and later at the funeral parlor was indicative of a simple director/star relationship or if there was possibly more to the romance rumors than was being admitted.

Mary, her cold and untalented sister, Margaret, and mother, Charlotte Shelby, resided in Los Angeles off Wilshire Blvd. at 56 Fremont Place in a home that had once belonged to Mary Pickford. Two large stone lions stood guard at the mansion's front door and people in the movie industry came to refer to these statues as "Charlotte" and "Margaret." The young star herself was known as "Hollywood's Lonely Princess," the moniker arising from the fact that her calculating mother, even during Mary's late teens, would not allow the girl much of a social life. Following a day's work at the studio, Mary was whisked home for an early bedtime since the lack of a full night's sleep might affect her yet untouched features and ultimately shorten her ability to support her parasitic family. It was said around town that, to maintain the actress' "little girl" image, Charlotte Shelby forced her daughter to dress as a child and keep her bedroom filled with dolls.

After a three hour session with the girl, Adams issued an official statement in which he said: "*Detective Sgts. Cato and Cahill, together with myself, interviewed Miss Minter. We talked with her for several hours regarding her relationship with Taylor. We are absolutely satisfied that she knows nothing that will throw any light at all on this mystery, nor do we believe that she is even remotely connected with the case.*"

Actor Lew Cody, known around Hollywood as a possible suitor to Mabel Normand, was also being investigated. It was asserted that the performer recently had a bitter quarrel with Taylor due to jealousy over the actress' affections. Adding to the interest of the police was the fact that Cody, who'd starred with Gloria Swanson back in 1919 in *Don't Change Your Husband*, fit the general description of the man Mrs. MacLean saw departing Taylor's bungalow, and he frequently wore dark silk scarves and a cap.

The actor was taken to Alvarado Street where the witness was afforded the opportunity of seeing him repeat the movements of her mysterious stranger, as he'd left Taylor's quarters. But, Mrs. MacLean was positive Cody was not the man. By the end of the day, he'd adequately accounted for his whereabouts on Wednesday night and was released.

Still another player, Tony Moreno, serial star for Vitagraph, was questioned that Saturday. Later, in his apartment at the Los Angeles Athletic Club, he made a public statement: "*I played golf with Mr.*

Taylor exactly a week before his death. We drove to the San Gabriel Country Club and remained there from about noon 'til dark. While there, I introduced him to Asa Keyes, the Deputy District Attorney.

"Wednesday night Mr. Taylor called me at the club. We discussed some business that I wanted him to participate in. As near as I can recall it, it was about seven o'clock when he called and he appeared to be in the best of spirits.

"After the call, I went to the club dining room and stayed there for dinner. The next morning I heard that Mr. Taylor was dead."

Edward Sands wasn't the only individual to be sought by police Saturday as a material witness. "Dapper Dan" Collins, wanted in New York City for the 1921 murder of wealthy manufacturer John H. Reid, was suggested as a possible participant in the crime when one astute investigator implied that one of the mysterious two cars seen around the Taylor bungalow on the night of the murder might have belonged to this man who police of more than one nation had termed the "master blackmailer of the century." Collins had been known to be operating as recently as last August in the Hollywood area—working with an unnamed motion picture star in a blackmail plot. Authorities weren't accusing Collins of specific complicity in the murder, since Sands, experts having proven it was his handwriting on the Fresno/Sacramento pawn tickets, was still the prime suspect. Yet, they felt that, considering his contacts in the picture industry and, especially, with the underworld, Collins might be able to give some help in solving the case.

Conceivably, blackmail could have figured prominently in the Taylor affair. The dead man's now revealed past was certainly not the most honorable. Sands was aware of his employer's "skeletons" and it's possible that he was extorting money by threatening exposure. Yet, if this was indeed the case and the valet was successful in his demands, why would he ultimately resort to burglary and forgery? And, why kill someone who was paying?

All Hollywood personalities were afraid of scandal; lest it destroy a career they'd worked so hard to build. They were, therefore, fair game to blackmailers who might threaten to expose damaging secrets of their past—whether they were true or false. Many of the victims acquiesced to a criminal's flagrant demands, while others refused to cooperate.

A member of the latter group was Mabel Normand who, in 1916, caused the arrest of Dr. Raymond A. Swett, charging him with attempted blackmail. Two city detectives, who had recorded Swett's demand for $610 on a dictograph, trapped the dentist in Miss Normand's apartments. After the blackmailer was arrested, he sent a note to the star in which he pleaded for the sake of his wife and children, not to press charges. Sympathetic to his plight, Miss Normand agreed and the matter was officially dropped. The secret the dentist was using as a threat was never revealed to the press.

Before he quit work on Saturday, Captain Adams put himself out on a limb by declaring that an arrest would be made in the Taylor case within twenty-four hours: "*Working secretly and while the suspected murderer believed that suspicion was falling on another person, detectives from my office have woven a chain of evidence that we believe is unbreakable. The net of evidence about this man is tightening like the tentacles of a deep-sea monster. The motive has been established, the activities of the suspect have been checked on the night of the murder, and the detectives will locate his hiding place easily when the links of the chain are complete. A woman may have been and possibly was the indirect cause of the crime, but no woman directed the murder in this case.*"

The subject of Adams' announcement remains a mystery, since his predicted arrest was never to take place.

Away from the police investigation, other events transpired on Saturday, which made interesting, although not sensational, news copy.

A statement issued by Mrs. Ethel Robins (Taylor's ex-wife) in New York reaffirmed the information about the director's early life which Ada Deane-Tanner had issued on Friday: "*Two and a half years ago, I discovered that Mr. Deane-Tanner had become William Desmond Taylor. I have no further statement that could possibly be of interest. The news of Mr. Deane-Tanner's death was a great shock to my daughter* (Ethel Daisy was then nineteen years old) *and me.*"

On the local front, in an effort to salvage something of the director's once spotless reputation, Ted Taylor of Famous Players publicity issued a hastily written press release in which he attributed Deane-Tanner's disappearance to the fact that he'd been shanghaied to the Orient and subsequently was the victim of amnesia. The announcement had received a hearty laugh in the *Dispatch*'s city room.

Another dispatch, this one from Denver, had a judge by the name of Ben B. Lindsey theorizing that Taylor might have been the victim of mistaken identity. Many years before, the director was held in jail for a night when the Denver police believed he was a wanted criminal. Taylor's protestations of innocence brought him nothing but a severe beating by police clubs. The following morning, after he'd established his identity, profuse apologies were extended, but the innocent man never learned the name of the fugitive for whom he was mistaken.

As Judge Lindsey put it: *"Was Taylor murdered for revenge by some crook whom his double had betrayed? He may have been the image of some underworld character?"*

Out of Seattle came recollections of some old sourdoughs of the Klondike gold rush. They said that Taylor was in Dawson City just before the turn-of-the-century with a "sister" who played the banjo. For a time, they worked in the community's vaudeville houses, after which proprietor "Arizona" Charlie Meadows hired Taylor as producer/stage director of the Standard Theatre stock company.

Word came out of Telluride, Colorado, that Taylor had worked as a night clerk there for six months (June-December 1910) at the New Sheraton Hotel. This information was offered via wire from the manager of that inn, who recalled the slain director was of exemplary character, read much of his spare time, avoided the associations of women, and, while brooding of his then low financial status, "was determined to make good." He made many friends during his stay in the mining town to whom he told the story of how he had been forced to seek the hotel position because of his heavy gambling losses at the roulette wheel that left him penniless.

When he departed Telluride on December 15, 1910, he informed his employer that he was going to Los Angeles to visit his dying brother and to collect an inheritance.

Could this brother have been the missing Dennis Deane-Tanner? If so, there would be a record of his death at the Los Angeles Hall of Records. And, what was this about an inheritance?

The Motion Picture Directors' Association had taken charge of funeral arrangements for Taylor and announced that services would be held at St. Paul's Pro-Cathedral at 2 p.m. on Tuesday, February 7. Dean MacCormack was to officiate.

I'd just completed my lengthy phone conversation with Sandy Haines when I received a visitor. Al Drebin, who never observed the Sabbath, was bright and cheerful with another "stop the presses" story. Al was a lonely bachelor and often dropped in around dinnertime for a chat. He was always welcome. I poured him a slug of first-rate bootleg scotch, then he commandeered my favorite chair from which to relate his news.

Along with Captain Adams and Officers Cato, Winn, and Cline, Al had been reexamining the scene at Taylor's 404-B South Alvarado bungalow when Mabel Normand paid them a visit.

"I guess she'd come directly from the inquest," said Al. "She was fantastic—very friendly, a real nice person. She said she wanted to see the house where 'Bill' lived again.

"Since she was there, we asked if she'd mind reenacting her last visit with Taylor and she said okay. So, she went through the whole thing and even showed us where that overturned chair belonged."

"What's the big deal about that?" I asked.

"The 'big deal,' Ben-a-la, is what happened next. She told us she wanted to reclaim some letters and telegrams she'd sent to Taylor, since their contents were somewhat personal and, if the press got hold of them, their meaning could be misconstrued."

"Did you give them to her?"

"Well, she led us upstairs to Taylor's bureau where she knew the letters were because he'd shown them to her."

I chuckled. "I thought they were just 'pals.' What the hell was she doing in his bedroom?"

"Probably fucking. Do you want to hear this or not?"

I did want to hear the story, so I shut up.

"Anyway, we opened the top drawer and there was nothing... *no letters*. We searched the whole goddamned bureau and didn't find a thing."

"Could the Public Administrator have taken them when he was doing the inventory?"

"Bryson? I doubt it. We couldn't reach him this afternoon, but we spoke to his assistant and the letters weren't on the list of inventoried items. We even called Eyton, the studio manager who helped Bryson go through the stuff. He didn't know about any letters either."

"So," I asked, "what happened to them?"

"I haven't the slightest idea," shrugged Al, who then pondered my question for a moment. "What was that you were saying the other day about monogrammed panties?"

Carol was perturbed with me. It was Sunday, our day to relax and do something together. In warm weather, we'd take in a ball game or drive out to the beach for a picnic. During the chilly months, there'd be a movie to see, an art gallery to visit. But, not today. Today, I was too wound up in the Taylor case to enjoy myself. In fact, I was thriving on it. I decided to check with the office (I'd called in the news of the missing Mabel Normand letters last night), then do some leg work.

Al and I were pretty well convinced that somebody was snatching potential evidence to protect either himself or a friend from public scandal. That's what everybody in the movies feared most these days. First, the undergarments disappeared, then the "S" monogrammed handkerchief, although I'd come to question whether that item ever existed in the first place. More likely, an eager detective, wanting to close the net around Sands, had manufactured that fact. Not an unusual police practice in 1922.

And now, Mabel's letters had followed suit.

On the surface, it seemed like a couple of very famous actresses were probably having affairs with Taylor and, as Al tendered, a studio executive (Eyton?) might simply be protecting the reputations of its personalities and thereby the company's financial interest in them.

Miss Normand was not contracted to Famous Players, but the studio still had some of Taylor's unreleased pictures on the shelf. Bad publicity about the director, if wife abandonment was not enough, could certainly hurt their chances at the box-office.

It was Al's intent to question Charles Eyton more thoroughly. He had ample opportunity to search Taylor's bungalow Thursday morning before the authorities took charge. And, he'd been most helpful in assisting the Public Administrator with his inventory. Most helpful, indeed.

For my part, I decided not to tell Al of my suspicions about Ike St. Johns and the vanishing undergarments until I'd had an opportunity to confront the mayor's press secretary myself. Ike knew me as an honorable reporter and was more likely to be completely open in a private off-the-record conversation with a colleague than in an official investigation by a police sergeant. Also, anything he told Al would, eventually, be given out to the other papers, although Al would give me a couple hours lead time if he could, and I wanted the story *exclusive*.

My wife announced that she was going to spend Sunday with me whether I worked or not. A moment's thought on the matter, and I agreed. Why not let her see how her "better" half spent his day?

The city room was staffed with the usual Sunday skeleton crew. With all city agencies and private businesses closed, there was no need to have a full complement of people working. 5' 4" Nate Barker was on the desk as Sunday Editor, so not even Andy Lundy worked today.

Nate was a friendly sort who didn't let his small stature bother him too much. He lacked Lundy's astute sense of commercial journalism, but since Sunday was usually uneventful, there was always a rather relaxed atmosphere around the office and any experienced rewrite/make-up man like Barker could put together the paper quite adequately.

He gave us a warm smile as Carol and I entered the city room, leaving his desk to come over and greet us—or, at least *her* since the pseudo editor considered himself quite the ladies' man, especially when the girl, like Carol, was his size or shorter. I cleared my throat or made some such sound and Nate shifted his attention to me.

"What's new on the Taylor story?" I asked.

"Not a hell of a lot," he replied, walking back to his chair with me tagging along behind. In the meantime, Carol amused herself by sitting at my desk and reading my bylined story in the early edition: 'WHERE ARE MABEL'S LETTERS???'

Nate thumbed through several scraps of newsprint.

"We have another sighting of Sands within a block of Taylor's place right after the murder. Witness' name is Malden, some sort of studio stagehand.

"Police questioned a cameraman this morning. Some guy at Famous Players called them when he heard this fellow say 'Bill Taylor got only what he deserved!' Evidently, the cameraman showed up for work drunk one day and Taylor fired him."

"Anything to it?"

"Nothing. Waste of time."

"What else?"

"They're still chasing drug peddlers, hoping that might lead somewhere." He referred to his notes. "And, some 'prominent young New York man,' who was formerly connected with an actress involved in the case, is being sought. He's supposed to have checked out of his hotel the day of the murder and hasn't been seen since. The police think he might be in Mexico."

"Who's the man?"

"They won't say, but Jerry Grant thought it might be Thomas Dixon, Jr. of the pencil manufacturing Dixons. He used to date Mary Miles Minter."

"No, he didn't!" piped in my wife who'd been eavesdropping. "Colleen Moore use to go out with him. Mary only left the house with Tommy Dixon. He was rich and that's why her mother approved of him. Her *real* date was Marshall Neilan, who'd pick up Colleen, then they'd all meet later at wherever they were going and switch dates."

"Mickey" Neilan was the director of an almost unbroken string of box-office hits (*Daddy Long Legs* with Mary Pickford; *Dinty*, starring Colleen Moore; *Bits of Life* with Lon Chaney; and *The Lotus Eater*, starring John Barrymore) and, like Bill Taylor, had quite a reputation with members of the opposite sex.

"Are you sure about that?" I asked.

Carol flashed her smug grin. "What do you think we secretaries do all day around the studio? Work?"

Nate and I both chuckled. "Frankly," he ventured, "I don't think he's a serious suspect. Cops are just checking him out like they have everybody else."

He read a statement Grant had taken from Captain Adams this morning: "*We have gone through a great mass of matter, documentary, and otherwise. We have interviewed scores of people and we have been able to set aside many theories and suspicions as inapplicable. We are confident that the clearing away of the nonessentials will lead us, before long, to the absolutely correct hypothesis, and from that to the discovery and arrest of the murderer.*"

Apparently, the good Captain had retreated somewhat from his staunch stand of yesterday where he'd predicted that the killer's arrest would take place within twenty-four hours.

"You could sure use a stronger headline story for the next edition," I suggested to Nate.

"You're telling me. I thought we might go with either 'SANDS SPOTTED AT MURDER SCENE,' or 'NEW YORK MAN SOUGHT.'"

"Nobody's been able to interview Mrs. MacLean yet," I said. "All we've got from her is what the police or her husband has told us second-hand. It's Sunday. Why don't I run over there and see what I can come up with. If I'm lucky, I'll call you before the late edition goes to bed."

Nate liked my idea. He had to, since there was nothing very substantial for the front page of the next edition otherwise. Carol and I departed for Alvarado Street, after which we planned to take in a movie.

The bungalow court was not without visitors on this peaceful Sunday afternoon. Tourists wandered in off the street to gawk at the murder site that they'd been reading about in their newspapers for the past few days. Taylor's bungalow had been chain-locked and a sign was prominently displayed stating the quarters were still under investigation by the police.

We bypassed the amateur photographers and headed straight for the MacLean apartment. Faith Cole MacLean answered the door herself, as it was the servant's day off and her husband, Douglas, was out on the golf course. She was an attractive woman, a former New York socialite with much more charm and class than the average housewife.

"I'm sorry," she said, after I'd introduced myself, "but I prefer not to give any newspaper interviews."

"Gee, Mrs. MacLean," I said, trying to make my boyish features work in my favor as they had in the past, "I really wish you'd reconsider. My editor is putting a lot of pressure on me to get this interview and, if I don't, he may fire me. I couldn't really afford that right now. You see, my wife is expecting a baby...."

I caught Carol's dirty look out of the corner of my eye, but the ruse appeared to be working; not that the comedian's wife believed me necessarily. She simply admired my *chutzpah*.

"All right," she chuckled, "come in and I'll talk to you for a few minutes."

She led us into her elegant Spanish-décor living room, inviting us to be seated on the sofa. Taking out my notepad, I asked her to go over her story for me so I could use her own words.

"We had dinner about seven o'clock," she began, "and finished about a half hour later. The gas heater wasn't working properly, so Mr. MacLean went upstairs to see if he could fix it. While he was gone, I heard what must have been the shot that killed Mr. Taylor. I wasn't sure it was really a shot at all, but I distinctly heard an explosion. That was, I'd say, around ten minutes to eight." She pointed to the window that filled the living room wall. "I went to the window and saw this man leaving the Taylor apartment."

"Describe him, please."

"I gave this all to the police," she protested slightly, then continued. "I should say he was about 5' 9," wore a muffler and cap, and he might have had a prominent nose, but that impression might be because of the shadow from the arc lamp."

"Could it have been Edward Sands?"

"Absolutely not! Sands was a much heavier man."

The interview had not yet provided me with anything new, so I asked my hostess to attempt an experiment. "Mrs. MacLean, bear with me on this. Sit back, close your eyes, and try to visualize the man *exactly* as you saw him that night."

She gave me a curious look, but as she seemed to be enjoying our visit, decided to go along with my request. It was a moment before she spoke. "The man had already opened the door and was looking toward Alvarado Street."

"Did he seem to be in a hurry?"

"No, he was the coolest thing I have ever seen. He turned around, looked at me, smiled, and hesitated. Then it seemed to me that Mr. Taylor must have spoken to him from inside the house. The man pulled the door shut, turned around and, looking at me all the time, went down the couple of steps that go to Taylor's house and then went toward Maryland Street and the alley.

"He wasn't a well-dressed man, more like my idea of a motion picture burglar."

"What about distinctive features—his face, the way he walked?"

She was trying very hard to conjure up a vivid picture in her mind. "He was a funny-looking man. His face looked like it had, maybe, movie make-up on it.

"I suppose it was a man. He was dressed like a man—heavy coat, muffler wound around his chin, and a cap pulled way down over his eyes...."

"Go on," I prodded.

"But he almost walked like a woman and had the build of a woman, quick little steps and broad hips and short legs."

I was excited now. "You mean, it could have been a woman dressed like a man?"

"It might have been," she said slowly, turning the thought over in her mind.

"If, in fact, it was a woman, who do you think it might have been?"

"I really don't know." She hesitated and I'm positive that in that instant she, at least, thought she knew who the person might have been. "I'm sorry," she said, a bit agitated now, "I can't tell you anything else."

It was obvious that the interview was at an end. I thanked her and asked if I might use the hall phone to call my paper. Again she was gracious and, while I phoned Nate Barker, she and Carol chatted.

"Nate," I said, "here's your headline: DID A WOMAN KILL TAYLOR?"

Carol was really steamed after we'd left the MacLean residence. She didn't appreciate that I'd lied and used her presence to get that interview. "Look, honey," I explained, "you wanted to come along. Well, it's my job to uncover news. Sometimes I have to use less than honorable means and that's too bad. I'm sorry if I upset you, but I got a damn good story and that's the name of the game."

We didn't talk much the rest of the day.

Ike St. Johns was a hard man to see, but I finally cornered him first thing Monday morning. It was an easy accomplishment, since I'd been waiting at his City Hall parking space since 7:45.

"Hiya, Ben," he said, a courteous smile gracing his near-classic features. "You're here early, aren't you?"

"Only way it seems I can talk to you, Ike."

He glanced at his watch. "I've got to be in the mayor's office in ten minutes. What's up?"

"I want to know what happened to those panties. The monogrammed ones."

"What panties?" he said, a bit taken aback.

"Come on, Ike. You know what I'm talking about. What did you do with those panties that were in Taylor's bureau? I saw them there before Cahill threw me out of the bedroom."

"Ben, I don't know what you're talking about."

He tried to move past me, but I grabbed him by the arm.

"Damn it!" I was getting mad now. "Don't walk away! I could have told the police what I know, but I didn't. Now, if you don't level with me, that's the next place I go."

He knew I wasn't kidding. "Ben, look…."

"I promise that, if you want, the conversation stays off the record until you tell me otherwise."

Ike knew that I was a man of my word; so it didn't take him long to decide. "There *were* some monogrammed panties. I stuck them in my briefcase because I didn't want the initials to wind up in the papers. I think they belong to... well, a very famous actress. You know what it would do to her career if her affair was publicized."

"What were the initials?"

"Forget it. That, I don't tell. But, rest assured, the proper authorities have been informed and, if it develops she was involved in the murder, which I really don't think was possible, then you'll know in good time."

He put his hand on my shoulder. "Ben, you're a reasonable reporter, maybe one of the best in town. You don't want to hurt this innocent."

Of course I didn't, but for the sake of my gnawing curiosity, I had to know. "Ike," I said, thinking of the blonde hairs I wasn't supposed to know about, were the initials 'M'?"

"No comment," he retorted. He walked away, into the building.

No leads of any real significance were developed on Monday. The unnamed "prominent New York man" (Dixon, Jr.?) was located in a downtown Los Angeles hotel by sheriff's deputies, questioned for two hours, and then released when his alibi checked.

The afternoon brought an urgent wire to the L.A.P.D. from the Constable of Carlin, Nevada, in which that small town official reported a man answering the description of Edward Sands had been in his jurisdiction for several days. Further investigation proved that the man was not the fugitive valet. Two days later, somebody else thought they spotted Sands, this time in Lowell, Arizona. They, too, were mistaken.

Detective Captain David Adams decided to make another of his "profound" public statements on Monday: *I am now completely convinced that Sands is the man we want. I believe it was he who committed the crime and he will be formally charged within the next forty-eight hours. We have many established important facts which enable us to reconstruct the crime with what we believe is absolute accuracy. Experiments made by our own and outside gun experts demonstrate beyond question that the shot which killed Taylor was fired from a dis-*

tance of not more than an inch or two from his body. We have made many tests with the coat he was wearing, and in the test that produced a hole similar to that already appearing in the coat, the muzzle of the revolver was held an inch from the garment. When Taylor was shot, he had his left arm up. We believe that the murderer ordered 'hands up' and shot him when he obeyed his command."

Al Drebin's reaction to Adams' statement was, "He's kidding himself. We got nothing more concrete on Sands than we had two days ago. Captain's under a lot of pressure to solve this thing, but right now he's just whistling in the dark."

"By the way, Al," I said before we concluded the phone call, "you saw, I'm sure, my interview with Mrs. MacLean?"

"You're not very popular down here," he laughed, "with the boys that questioned her first time around. They got their butts chewed this morning."

"A suggestion," I said. "Go back out and talk to her again. It's just a hunch, but I think she may know who that mysterious man or woman is, and for some reason, she's not talking."

"I'll tell you," he said, "all these movie people are clamming up on this one."

Anytime you have an unsolved criminal case, be it murder, kidnapping, robbery, or what-not, both the police department and the press are going to receive an overabundance of information and leads, most of it utterly useless, from the local citizenry. The Taylor mystery was no different. The *Dispatch*, as well as the other papers in Los Angeles, the nation, and the world, maintained the story on the front page for as long as it kept circulation high. Our phones continually rang with "leads" as to the whereabouts of Sands, theories on the murder itself, and the spotting of Mrs. MacLean's mysterious stranger. Indeed, it seemed that any man dressed in a cap and muffler, rather common attire during the chilly month of February, was suspect. Many of these informants were honest concerned citizens attempting to offer what they thought might be valuable clues. On the other hand, I can't recall the number of people, mostly unknown actors seeking publicity, who claimed that prior to the murder, they were approached on the street by the "cap and muffler man" and asked, "Where does William Desmond Taylor live?"

I began to wonder if the late director had thrown a party and forgot to put his address on the invitations.

Nevertheless, one of the earliest and most bizarre of these stories to come to light was through Sam Cooper of the Yellow Cab Company. I'd done a feature story on that firm some months back and, since then, Cooper had always thrown me any news leads he'd come across. You'd be surprised at the number of front-page stories that have developed from a conversation or incident in a taxi.

Monday was half over when the assistant general manager of the cab company phoned and told me that one of his drivers, a young man named C.M. Meister, had an interesting tale to relate that might be tied up with the Taylor affair. We met in a small coffee shop across the street from the company's main office.

Meister was in his early twenties. His sincerity convinced me that the experience he related actually occurred, but whether it was connected to the Taylor case or not was another matter altogether.

"On last Wednesday night," he began, "at 10:55, I picked up four passengers at 620 South Broadway, two men and two women. Upon entering the cab, one of the men pulled up the window between them and me, so apparently I might not hear the conversation. I drove them to an address in the Wilshire District. One of the men and the women left the cab and went into the apartment house. The other man remained in the cab and asked me to drive him to the Ambassador Hotel. I did so, and he was in the hotel for about fifteen minutes. He came out carrying a leather briefcase. Shortly after he re-entered the cab, he appeared to show the greatest anxiety concerning the briefcase. He handed it to me and said, 'I want you to deliver that. For God's sake, don't lose it.' His order to me was to 'drive to 400 South Rampart Street.' At least, that was the number I caught. There was a 400 in it, but I'm not sure if it was an even number."

Rampart Street is not far from Alvarado.

"He asked me several times if the briefcase was safe," Meister continued, "and, finally, he took it from me and put it on the seat beside him. When we reached a streetcar stop, he decided to get out and take the car and asked me to deliver the briefcase to a woman who'd be waiting.

"Immediately upon my arrival at the address, the woman rushed out of the apartment and asked if I had the briefcase. Just then, a man wearing a muffler came running from the side of the house—the same man I'd let out with the women. He got into the cab and told me to drive around the block a few times, and then return to the apartment house.

"This I did, but when we got back, there was a roadster in front. My passenger became very excited and shouted, 'Don't let them see me! Drive around again!' He fell to the floor in the back and didn't get up until we pulled up at the apartment again and found the car gone. He got out, paid me, and said, 'I was a damned fool to do that thing.'"

I didn't know what to make of Meister's story. Maybe his passengers had been involved in a blackmail deal and were transporting the booty, or perhaps they could be dope dealers delivering a shipment. On the other hand, there could be some perfectly innocent explanation for their behavior.

Whatever the situation, I doubted, as did the police when they investigated it further without results, that the strange incident was tied in with the Taylor case since his slaying had taken place nearly three hours earlier.

The day's most interesting news regarding Taylor was to emerge from the lips of my dear wife, who came home from the studio Monday night with a wealth of information.

Word was going around the Lasky lot that a dope pusher named Loper had been warned by Taylor to keep away from the studio. The peddler ignored the warning, and then about three weeks ago, the director had caught him selling his wares, and had beaten him severely. Perhaps the murder had been a revenge killing?

The discussion of narcotics was, indeed, a popular one with the gossips. Names like Wallace Reid, one of the screen's most handsome leading men, Alma Rubens (she'd been sensational in *Humoresque*), and even Mabel Normand had been mentioned—sans concrete evidence—as possible users.

How these prominent personalities got started on drugs—if they were, in fact, on them at all—was a mystery, although the popular story going around was that there was a rather personable character actor who, when his fellow workers complained of a hangover or the like, would offer them a fix to make them feel better.

Speaking of Mabel, several studio personnel recalled that she and Taylor had a very loud argument the previous New Year's Eve when they'd attended a party at the Alexandria Hotel. Some said he became angry at her because she'd had too much to drink (Mabel had a reputation for enjoying her alcohol) and was flirting with other men, while people with more sordid imaginations claimed it started over her supposed narcotics habit, which the director had been attempting to break her of.

The comedienne had told Taylor that his "phony dignity" sickened her and, after he'd entreated her not to be so "melodramatic," the pair left together. Close friends of the director said he'd been in a state of depression for several days after the row.

Then, there was the reported meeting on the Friday night following the murder at Marshall Neilan's home. Mabel was there, as were Gloria Swanson, Actor Jack Pickford, and others. The director was supposed to have advised Miss Normand that the only way she would be able to come out of this scandal with her career intact was to cooperate fully with the authorities.

"Panic" had been the key word around the studios these past few days. With the nation's less responsible papers enlarging on the truth and printing every shabby rumor as if it were fact, the reform groups were crying for "blood." Tales that a number of producing firms were planning to abandon Hollywood and move their base of operations east were rife for many days and prompted the Chamber of Commerce of one small town outside Washington D.C. to invite, through Will Hays, the picture industry to move its activities to their quiet community.

Nevertheless, what created the most anxiety with the Famous Players family was the verified news that their president, Adolph Zukor, possibly the most powerful man in the industry, was on his way west, ostensibly to "clean house."

A British flag draped the coffin of William Desmond Taylor at his funeral, held on Tuesday, February 7, at St. Paul's. While a unit of uniformed police denied the throngs of curious spectators entry into the cathedral, Dean William MacCormack officiated at the services, which were attended by many of the slain director's "friends." Mabel Normand was there, but the strain proved to be too much for her and, after a few minutes, she fainted and was driven away in an ambulance. Henry Peavey was also in attendance—crying as hysterically as he'd done at the inquest.

Noticeably absent was Mary Miles Minter, although she, along with Miss Normand, Gloria Swanson, Rudolph Valentino, Wallace Reid, Thomas Meighan, Agnes Ayers, Jack Holt, Bebe Daniels, Dorothy Dalton, Betty Compson, and Douglas MacLeans, had sent a floral offering. Pallbearers included William DeMille, George Melford, Arthur Hoyt, Frank Lloyd, and Charles Eyton. There was also an honorary guard of pallbearers from the Overseas Club.

All in all, the Hollywood community gave Bill Taylor a pretty impressive send-off. One wouldn't have thought he had an enemy in the world.

10

olice in Miami, Florida, took master swindler "Dapper Dan" Collins into custody on Tuesday and, after hours of intensive questioning and verification of his movements, it was announced that he wasn't connected with the Los Angeles slaying in any way. He was held for extradition by New York authorities, who were seeking him on that old murder charge.

The same day, Howard Fellows, Taylor's chauffeur and younger brother of assistant director Harry Fellows, approached the Los Angeles investigators to tell them that *he* might be the mysterious stranger Mrs. MacLean saw. On the night of the murder, Howard phoned his employer at approximately 7:55 to see if his services would be needed that evening. Receiving no answer, the chauffeur went to the bungalow, arriving at 8:15. He rang the doorbell and, when there was no reply, put up Taylor's automobile for the night and walked home. He was wearing a cap and raincoat and, as far as he was concerned, was the man viewed by Faith Cole MacLean.

Mrs. MacLean, after being re-questioned, denied that Fellows could have been the man she'd seen. Aside from the fact that she knew Fellows, there was approximately a twenty-five minute discrepancy between the time she said she saw her stranger and when Fellows claimed he was on the premises. Also, the witness was positive that her "figure" had come *out* of the house.

Al Drebin, following my suggestion, was unable to get the woman to admit she recognized the probable killer, although he agreed with my conclusion that she possibly thought she knew who it was.

The police were baffled. Sure, they were making a lot of official noise for the benefit of the citizenry, but, none of the plethora of clues that had been uncovered in the six days since Taylor's body was found amounted to much in pinpointing the identity of his slayer. The "strong" case against Edward Sands was the best thing the cops had going for them and that evidence was still only circumstantial. The other so-called clues (published or otherwise) had not yet done anything but drag the name of the deceased, as well as several of his lady friends, through the mud. Yet, the authorities continued to release (or let slip) their scandalous tidbits in order to make it appear they were accomplishing something. As long as the newspaper reading public had sordid facts to speculate over during their morning and evening meals, the actual solution to the murder itself took a secondary position and, therefore, alleviated Adams and his cohorts of a great deal of pressure.

The good detective captain must have been delighted when, on Tuesday, one of his men discovered a letter in Taylor's quarters, not one of Normand's writings, but by the hand of another actress "admirer" of the late Englishman. Upon opening a book in the library, Detective Cato found the correspondence, written in a juvenile code and bearing the crest of "M.M.M." Its deciphered contents were definitely out-of-character for Hollywood's popular "sweet young *ingénue*," Mary Miles Minter, with the long blonde curls. The missive's public exposure in the *Dispatch* and the other papers of the world certainly helped sound the death knell for her thriving career.

I wish I could say I tried to stop my paper from printing the contents of the letter, but that's not true. Like all the other members of the fourth estate, I played it up for all it was worth, knowing very well we were dealing with the outpourings of an unhappy, immature little girl. I justified it to myself by employing my own phraseology, "The public has a right to know."

A portion of the letter:

What shall I call you, wonderful man? I want to go away with you—up in the hill—anywhere—just so we can be alone.

I would sweep and dust—oh, yes, and fix the table and help you wash the dishes, and then, in my spare time, darn the socks.

I'd go to my room and put on something scant and flowing; then I would lie on the couch and wait for you. I might fall asleep, for fire makes me drowsy. Then, I would wake and find two strong arms around me and two dear lips pressed to mine in a long sweet kiss.

Dearest, I love you. I love you. I love you. XXXX
Yours always,
Mary

Supplementing this was news from a San Francisco paper that, in December of 1919, Mary Miles Minter was in the Bay City to address the San Francisco Advertising Club. She was registered at the St. Francis. Staying at the same hotel was William Desmond Taylor.

Al Drebin had met with Lasky General Manager Charles Eyton following the funeral and informed him of his suspicions regarding the fate of the Mabel Normand letters. Although, as Al explained to me later, he "really put the screws to that *macher.*" Eyton continually, if nervously, denied any knowledge of what Al was seeking. (The *Dispatch* and several other papers whose staff's had put "two and two together," had been surmising in print since Saturday that the manager, without mentioning him by name, had indeed taken the potential evidence to protect the interests of Famous Players-Lasky,)

Yet, the next day, the correspondence turned up as mysteriously as it had vanished, found by Cato in the toe of one of Taylor's riding boots. How they got there, nobody really knew for sure.

February 8th was the day that Los Angeles District Attorney Thomas Lee Woolwine officially entered the investigation to "counsel and advise" (actually, he took charge). Considered by his peers as an honest, fearless prosecutor with a strong sense of "Western justice," some years before, Woolwine had brought about the recall of Los Angeles Mayor Harper and the resignation of other officials, including the police commissioner, after making charges of vice protection against them. Currently, he was beginning his prosecution of the Madalynne Obenchain case. She, along with Arthur C. Burch, was accused of the murder of J. Belton Kennedy in the Beverly Glen area of the county.

From the standpoint of justice, Woolwine's move, with the backing of Mayor Cryer, to take a more active interest in the Taylor case was a proper one. As a responsible public official, he'd become disgusted with the "fun and games" the papers had been having with the peripheral facts of the murder, which, in his view, was not closer to being solved than it had been a week ago. Newspaper editorials, including one by Andy Lundy in the *Dispatch*, had intimated that Hollywood personnel were only telling half-truths about their knowledge of the case in order to protect themselves and their industry. Suggestions were made that the D.A. might be able to garner better results than the police.

Woolwine had an excellent staff of investigators at his disposal and immediately assigned one of his best, Ed C. King, to head up the revitalized probe.

On a purely selfish level, I wasn't too happy with this switch. I didn't have an informant like Al Drebin in the D.A.'s office and I knew that, from now on, I was going to have to work a little harder if I was going to get any "scoops" on the case.

The L.A.P.D. turned all information and evidence in their possession over to the District Attorney's office and indicated that they would be working along with that agency in solving the case. As Detective Sgt. Cline put it, "We were told that all information henceforth will be given out by W.C. Doran, Chief Deputy District Attorney. He has all the facts in our possession and has assumed command of the case."

The "marriage" was carried out very smoothly with no apparent ill words between the two public agencies. However, few observers couldn't help but notice the slight remains of egg on the faces of the Los Angeles cops.

Doran immediately announced that all people previously linked with the case would be rigidly questioned again—Mabel Normand; Mary Miles Minter; the Douglas MacLeans; Neva Gerber and Claire Windsor, both former girl friends of Taylor; Howard Fellows; and Henry Peavey were all to appear at the prosecutor's office within the next twenty-four hours.

Explaining the district attorney's position, Mr. Doran said: *"Edward Sands is certainly our principal suspect. However, no formal complaint is likely to be issued until we have a chance to examine several important witnesses who have shown a reticence to cooperate fully with us because the complete truth might hurt their professional position or interests.*

"The barricade of silence between the searchers for the truth and the truth itself is about to be broken."

11

"**M**r. Eyton will see you now," said the brunette secretary, opening the door to her boss' office for me. Famous Players' West Coast general manager had only kept me waiting about two minutes while he'd concluded a phone call. Evidently, Ted Taylor, of the studio publicity department, had suggested that he go above and beyond the call of duty to extend me every courtesy possible since the result of our interview could have somewhat of an effect on the public's future attitude toward the picture industry.

I'd called Ted after Doran had issued his "barricade of silence" statement with the suggestion that Charles Eyton might be receptive to talking candidly with a member of the press who would report the conversation objectively and also agree to treat any off-the-record statements as such. The publicist had been enthusiastic about the idea. His recent efforts to present Hollywood in an angelic light had not been too successful, so he was grateful for any aid he could get. An hour after we talked, he'd phoned back, telling me to come in at nine the next morning (Thursday).

Eyton, a rather large man in his fifties, greeted me with a warm handshake and a wary smile, then invited me to sit across the desk from him in his attractively, but practically, furnished office. There was some small talk—he knew Carol, she was a nice girl, a good employee—before he got down to the reason I was there.

"Mr. Birnbaum," he replied to my first inquiry, "that's a pretty obvious question. You really want to know why people like myself or Mabel Normand or Mack Sennett are reticent to give candid statements to the press?"

I nodded.

"So, let's put the *tuchis* right on the table. There's no 'conspiracy of silence' in Hollywood. We're just trying to protect ourselves from the irresponsibility of reporters, present company excepted, of course."

"Thank you," I replied, giving him a polite smile.

"Although I must admit," he continued, feeling he couldn't let me off scot-free, "I wasn't too happy with your story about the Mary Minter letters."

"That was officially given out to the press by the police," I said. "As a newspaperman, it was my job to report the facts to the public."

He started pacing the room. "Of course. I really have no quarrel with you on that. But, it's the bastards who make up their stories or base them strictly on wild rumors that are destroying this business."

Picking up some clippings from his desk, he began to quote: "'If you knew, if I could only tell the horrors that I know of this dreadful place. . .'That's from a Chicago sheet. Another paper said that we, in Hollywood, give our babies shots of heroin every night to keep them from crying and that the women's morals in this town were 'unspeakable.' That's the kind of thing I mean. Here's a New York paper that claims there is only one movie star in all of Hollywood who has *not* taken a drug cure...."

"Who's that?" I quipped.

It took a moment before he realized that I was trying to test his sense of humor. He chuckled, knowing that I was, indeed, sympathetic to his plight. Returning to his chair, he assumed a quieter tone.

"You don't know the damage those Mary Minter letters have caused. We were supposed to open *Tillie*, her new picture, in Lynn, Massachusetts, this week. Well, it's been cancelled. Some church group protested to the local censorship committee and they, in turn, got the theater owner to pull the film.

"The way this case is going, that sort of thing is liable to happen all over the country. Hell, we've got a lot of money tied up in that project—and in Miss Minter. Can't you see what this kind of journal-ism…?"

"It's called 'yellow journalism,'" I piped in, "and, to the best of my knowledge, the *Dispatch* has never practiced it.

"Look, Mr. Eyton, as I told Ted Taylor when I spoke to him, I think that an on-the-level interview with you right now could be very helpful to your situation. Let me throw some of these circulating rumors at you—one-by-one—and you tell me if there's any merit to them. The public should appreciate your honest replies."

"All right. Go ahead and ask." The game of cat and mouse had begun.

"Did you take the Normand letters?"

"If I did, I'd be pretty foolish to admit it, wouldn't I? Even off-the-record."

"I imagine so."

"But, let's talk hypothetically for a minute. Let's just *suppose* that I did take the letters. My only reason for doing so would be to see that the press didn't crucify innocent people. Any intimacies Miss Normand, or anybody else for that matter, shared with Bill Taylor are really not the public's business."

"Even if they provide a clue to his killer's identity? A motive, maybe?"

"There was nothing in those letters that…." Eyton smiled, realiz-ing that he had not taken the time to choose his words carefully. "I'm sure that *whoever* took those letters would not have done so if he, for one minute, thought he was obstructing justice. After he had an op-portunity to read the correspondence and see that there was nothing scandalous contained within, he simply returned them as quietly as possible. Morally speaking, I don't think it's wrong to try to save the reputation of a lady… or a gentleman." The manager stared at me for a minute, and we both knew who his "hypothetical" person was.

"Tell me, Mr. Eyton, who do you think killed Taylor?"

"How should I know? I'm not a detective. From the papers, I get the impression that the valet, Sands, did it. At least, that's what the police seem to think."

"Sands is too obvious," I said. "I have the feeling—as do certain members of the police force—that somebody is aiming all this incriminating evidence in his direction so the case can be solved quick-ly, and so the authorities won't look toward other areas for a solution to the crime, which they're starting to do now."

"Ridiculous!" said Eyton. "There was some woman who heard Sands threaten Bill the day before he was murdered."

"But, who was she?" I countered. "The wife of Taylor's ex-chauf-feur. Think about that. Chances are, if Earl Tiffany is seeking another job as a driver, that position will be found somewhere within the pic-ture business."

"You're suggesting that Mrs. Tiffany made up a tale to placate somebody in the industry?"

"It's possible. A person has to make good money to be able to afford a chauffeur."

He was getting upset again. "I don't believe this," he said. "You think that I or any other decent person in this business would be stupid enough to try and conceal a murder? Especially the murder of a man as popular as Bill Taylor? I don't care if the killer was Bill Hart, Chaplin, Mary Pickford, or whoever else suits your fancy. An entire industry is at stake here and *nobody* in a position of author-ity is going to jeopardize it by trying to save the guilty party. That would be insane. We've even hired our own detectives to work on the case."

"That's not what I'm referring to," I said, trying to quiet him. "It just seems to me that you and other studio executives would prefer that the police look elsewhere for their answers, rather than in your own backyard. It makes for better public relations.

"Sands is ideal for that purpose. He's only on the fringe of the industry and if he is guilty, everybody is home free… providing no other nasty skeletons have come to light through the investigation. And, the fact that everybody I or the police talk to close their mouths whenever we get to subjects aside from Sands makes one curious enough to want to explore those other closets. For example, how many stars are on dope?"

I'd put that question badly. He gave me a cold, determined look, which, I knew, signaled the end of our interview. "None that *I* am aware of."

I could have lingered a few more minutes, thrown a few specific names at him—like Famous Players' star, Wallace Reid. But, there were going to be no further replies of any substance. I thanked the harassed executive for his time and departed.

Back at the office, I read a statement Producer Samuel Goldwyn had issued from New York. The executives were certainly maintaining a solid front: "*A report that motion picture producers are attempting to suppress the true facts in the Taylor case would be too absurd to warrant comment were it not that many thousands of people will read the report and believe it as they have believed other false stories published about the motion picture industry.*

"*The motion picture industry comprises a population greater than that of almost any city in the world. No city ever gets through the year without any regrettable happenings. It is as unjust to say that the moving pictures need cleaning up as to speak of cleaning up the United States. The good and helpful things the industry is doing for the betterment of the world are never chronicled on the front page. But let anybody in the movies get into trouble and not only he, but the whole industry, is in the headlines for many days. When the industry was fortunate enough to secure so great an executive as Will H. Hayes for cooperation in its problems, the wildest rumors of political plans and fantastic statements that he was to be insured for $2 million were published everywhere. I cannot ask the newspapers to ignore the occurrences in so important an activity, but I do ask the public to read these stories in their true perspective and realize that the moving picture industry is made up of all sorts of people and that being a moving picture man or woman is no more an indication of character than being a plumber, a steel man, a banker, a merchant, or what not.*"

Goldwyn made sense and his tone certainly tempered the article I wrote about Charles Eyton.

12

The ugly idea of blackmail arose in everybody's thoughts again on Thursday when Investigator Ed King from the D.A.'s office and Public Administrator Frank Bryson made an interesting discovery: On January 31st, Taylor had written a check, payable to Cash, in the amount of $2,500 and negotiated it personally at the First National Bank. February 1st—the day of the murder—found him re-depositing the like cash sum back into his account.

Investigators began to speculate that the slain director had withdrawn the money to pay off a blackmailer, who was, possibly, threatening him with public exposure of his past life in New York. At the last minute, Taylor changed his mind and the enraged extortionist killed him.

Supporting this theory was the fact that, for a man who earned $40,000 per year and lived somewhat modestly, Taylor had a remarkably low bank balance. What happened to his money? Had it been paid to blackmailers?

Yet, one friend of Taylor had recalled to police that the director had once made the statement, "There's only one way to treat a blackmailer. Kill him!"

Perhaps he'd tried this approach, only to find the tables turned on him.

Early that afternoon, everybody's attention turned to Topeka, Kansas. Police there were holding one Walter R. Underwood, who they'd taken from a New York bound train, which had left Los Angeles on Monday evening. He'd been traveling under the name of Walter Maddox. When a fellow passenger noted he bore a resemblance to the published description of Edward Sands, the alarm was sounded and Underwood seized.

As it turned out, the man was, indeed, a fugitive, having embezzled over $1,000 from his employer, the Pacific Electric Railroad, prior to his departure from Los Angeles. However the man was *not* Sands. According to Topeka authorities, Underwood claimed to be a friend of the vanished valet and had attended *"many orgies of women, liquor, and dope in the Taylor bungalow at which Mabel Normand and other actresses were present. In fact, I was at a wild party with Sands a night or two—well, it was so wild and long drawn I don't recall exactly when it ended."*

It seemed like a good story, so I spent some time doing a local rundown on Mr. Underwood. Pacific Electric had employed him as a receiving cashier. A check of his former residences (the Fanta Apartments on Union and the Yorkshire Hotel at Seventh and Broadway) told me that he was a heavy drinker, apparently had no visitors, nor did he receive any mail. A few more calls proved that there was no truth to his Sands story. As far as anybody knew, Taylor had not seen Sands for months. So, what would the valet be doing at a party in his bungalow—a party that, in fact, never actually took place?

The next day, Underwood altered his story. He claimed that he had no actual knowledge of Sands or Taylor. All his "facts" had come from newspapers.

Before I went over to D.A. Woolwine's office where a late afternoon statement had been promised, I took a look at some of the shots Chubby Collins had snapped earlier in the day at Taylor's crypt. Press coverage had turned his tomb into a regular tourist attraction—with literally hundreds of gawkers gathered there to view his resting place.

Woowine and Doran had spent all day (and would continue until midnight) questioning witnesses: Verne Dumas, Director of the California-Mexico Oil Company, who was a neighbor of Taylor's and the third man to enter the house after the discovery of the dead body; Charles Maigne, a director for Famous Players-Lasky; Captain W.A. Robertson, formerly of the U.S. Army; and actor Arthur Hoyt. None provided the investigators with anything substantial, although they were able to enlighten them somewhat about the director's habits and his lifestyle, as well as furnishing them names of other associates.

Also questioned were the brothers, Harry and Howard Fellows, Charles Eyton, the Douglas MacLeans, Mabel Normand, Henry Peavey, and an unnamed gentleman friend of Edna Purviance, Taylor's neighbor, who newsmen speculated might be Charlie Chaplin.

A patrolman named Long told Woolwine that on the night following the murder, he spotted a man acting suspiciously near the Taylor home. Upon being detected, he fled, dropping two cigarette butts in the process, which the officer retrieved. These butts were later compared with cigarettes from Taylor's specially made private stock and found to be the same.

Doran summarized the testimony of the witnesses and then fielded some general questions. Actually, no new information was forthcoming from the session, but when asked specifically if Mrs. MacLean recognized the mysterious stranger, he reported, "We're still looking into that."

His most significant announcement of the day concerned the Normand correspondence: "The letters written by Mabel Normand to Mr. Taylor, and now in our possession, contain nothing bearing upon the crime or tending to offer any solution to the mystery."

Mabel Normand granted reporters another interview in her apartment on Friday, in the hope that a statement would, frankly, get the press off her back. She'd risen from a sickbed to meet with the newsmen and Mr. Waldron from Mack Sennett's company, entreated not to pressure her. For the two days since the funeral, the comedienne had been on the verge of collapse. Cameras were absolutely forbidden.

"You will not see the Mabel Normand you know on the screen," said Waldron. "This terrible case has played havoc with her nerves."

Mabel appeared in a negligee, her hair down her back in school-girl braids. She was pale and her voice trembled with emotion when she mentioned Taylor.

"I will talk freely with you and tell you everything I know about the case," she said. "I ask only one thing in return. Print truthfully what I say. So much that is untrue has been printed about me. There is no secret about any phase of my relations with Mr. Taylor. My letters to him I would gladly set before the world if the authorities care to do that. I have nothing to conceal."

She went on to tell how the letters were really a series of jests between the pair and gave an example: "'Dear Mabel, I know you are an awful busy woman and haven't much time to grant a poor duffer like me, but how about dinner Wednesday night and the Orpheum? Yours always, Billy.'"

Her reply: "'Dear Desperate Desmond, Sorry I cannot dine with you tomorrow, but I have a previous engagement with a Hindu prince. Some other time.'"

Miss Normand claimed she'd never expected to marry Taylor and had not quarreled with him on New Year's Eve (or any other time) at the Alexandria Hotel, as rumored. On that particular evening, she was with the Mahon Hamiltons at a private party.

She denied the nightdress found in Taylor's bungalow was hers. The other papers had, finally, picked up on that bit of news, speculating to great lengths as to who the owner of that frilly item could be. Mabel insisted that the only time she was alone with Taylor in his house was on the night he was murdered.

The remainder of the interview was simply a blow-by-blow description of that final meeting with Taylor, her story remaining exactly the same as she'd told it to us on February 3rd.

One point she was quite explicit about, "I have no jealous lovers!"

W.C. Doran questioned Mary Miles Minter, accompanied by her attorney, on Friday. As the press was later informed, the actress claimed that she had not seen Taylor since December 23rd, and prior to that not for three months. She had gone to see him two days before Christmas—near midnight—in order to say "goodbye."

On the night of the murder, she'd been staying at the home of her grandmother, Julia Miles.

According to Mary, she and Taylor would have married if he'd been younger. "*I have always known that this was just an exquisite chapter in my life that must necessarily be a brief one,*" she said. "*I couldn't bear to part with it. It was just a beautiful thing that seldom occurs in the world today as I see it, as it is forced upon me. It was simply a beautiful white flame. I had always been a reserved, very retiring young girl, and he was the first man and the only man who ever embodied all the glories of manhood in one private body. He represented that to me. He never, by look, by word, or by deed, gave me any reason to doubt any of my ideals that were placed in him absolutely.*"

A year later, she would announce publicly that they had, in fact, been engaged at the time of his death.

But, at the studio, Carol had come up with a contrary viewpoint. Taylor had directed Mary in four quite successful pictures and wags were speculating that there was definitely more than a simple director/star relationship there. When Charlotte Shelby got a hint that her daughter was smitten with this "father figure," she informed the studio that Taylor would *not* direct another of Mary's films and forbade the girl to see him again. Whether she obeyed her mother or not on that point was anybody's guess, but none of her subsequent films at Famous Players did as well financially as the ones she'd done with Taylor, and her movies released after his death were to do virtually no business at all.

Sandy Haines had followed-up the story out of Telluride, Colorado, in which a former associate of Taylor's recalled that the Brit had gone to Los Angeles to visit a dying brother. In checking at the Hall of Records, the young reporter did not find any death certificate filed for Dennis Deane-Tanner during the years 1910-1915.

The case took another turn toward the bizarre late Friday when Al Drebin phoned me to let me know that the police had received an anonymous letter, posted from Denver, in which it was charged that Edward Sands was, in reality, Taylor's missing brother, Dennis, and had murdered him as a result of a boyhood quarrel over a girl.

13

By Saturday, February 11, authorities had been investigating the murder of William Desmond Taylor for ten days and were no closer to solving it than when they began. Sure, they had clues and leads to check, but everybody was starting to realize at this point that much of what investigators were chasing was based on rumor, conjecture, claims of kooks, or false stories supplied by apprehended criminals wishing for a deal. Police were getting plenty of exercise running these things down, but the ultimate effect was akin to a dog chasing its own tail.

This week, I was grateful for the arrival of Saturday. Startling disclosures had come one on top of the other these past few days and I needed the time to ponder the events, to determine in my own mind what the viable aspects of the case actually were. The Fourth Commandment may not have set aside the Sabbath for the unraveling of murder mysteries, but that's precisely what I was trying to do.

The idea that Edward Sands was the long-missing Dennis Deane-Tanner was an intriguing one. Certainly it would explain how the vanished valet would be aware of his employer's previous identity and his less-than-honorable manner of terminating his marriage. On the other hand, if Dennis had borne a grudge against his older brother because of their youthful mutual affections toward a girl, then why had he waited so many years before doing his sibling in? That part of the argument didn't make much sense. We of the press may have emphasized the Sands/brother angle in our stories to sustain reader interest, but I was never fully convinced of its ultimate truth.

More and more, my instincts were telling me that the answer to the riddle lay within the nearly impregnable Hollywood community.

It's not that these film folk were involved in a *mass* conspiracy to conceal the murderer's identity, of which they were, most likely, themselves ignorant, but considering the national uproar the crime had already caused, they were fearful that the ultimate solution of the crime could open a new Pandora's Box of woes.

For example, if the slaying had been the work of a rumored drug dealer seeking revenge for the beating Taylor had given him, wouldn't the man's arrest be proof of some sort that narcotics were, in fact, circulating at the studios? And, once *that* was out in the open, which valuable stars would be "trampled" during the subsequent purge that would be necessary to "clean up" the business?

Or, if the angry unpaid blackmailer of conjecture *did* turn out to be the culprit, how much of his clientele and their dark secrets would be revealed once he was apprehended?

Should jealousy be the motive, then there would be a variety of possibilities. Maybe a suitor of one of Taylor's girlfriends had decided to rid himself of the competition. Or, perhaps one of the ladies could have discovered the director's amorous interests were not hers exclusively. "A woman scorned," as they say. Mrs. MacLean had admitted that her mysterious friend with the cap and muffler could have been a woman.

I'd have given a month's salary—well, possibly, a week's—to know who Faith Cole MacLean thought that person was.

Trying to get an honest interview from the picture folk seemed impossible, so I decided to try another approach. After years of working the police beat, Jerry Grant had developed a number of reliable contacts on the fringes of the Los Angeles underworld. If people close to Taylor had been doing business with drug dealers or a blackmail ring, then possibly word had gotten out and, for a reasonable gratuity, a "stool pigeon" would open up with what he knew.

I made a mental note to phone Grant first thing Sunday morning.

Meanwhile, Hollywood was getting into gear to do battle with the "yellow" methods of the press. Gossip columnists, friendlier to Tinseltown residents than other members of the press, were approached by studio higher-ups and requested to start a campaign to counteract the "dirt" stories that had been appearing on the nation's front pages. British-born Elinor Glyn, author of *Three Weeks*, agreed to write a series of articles to be published in the *New York Times*, as well as in England, which would relate her "positive" experiences in the West Coast picture colony.

"The problem with the movie industry," Mrs. Glyn would say, *"is that so many young people in it get rich suddenly. They are not taught control and it is hard for them to resist temptation. A young girl acts with a handsome young star all day long in emotional scenes, and when she gets through she is apt to think that her husband is an awful bore. But, I think that in a short time, you will see a vast improvement and that the standard will come up to that of the stage."*

A few "special" writers, hoping to find a market for their scenarios, were to do similar tasks as Mrs. Glyn for other domestic publications

Across the nation, public statements issued during the past few days by interested parties were taking a rather ominous tone. The Motion Picture Theater Owners of New York State, in convention at Albany, served notice on the stars of the industry by means of resolution they would have to lead clean and moral lives or the exhibitors would "wipe them from the screens of the country."

From Chicago, where he was tied up in business meetings, Universal's Carl Laemmle said that *"ninety percent of all personnel in the studios are all right. Others will have to get out."*

And, from that same city, Mary Pickford and Douglas Fairbanks lamented, *"All those accounts about movie people are so exaggerated. It really is a great pity. Motion picture people are so in the limelight and so maligned."*

Los Angeles Mayor George Cryer issued the following: *"If you take into consideration the number of people engaged in the picture industry, the prominence given to all their doings, even to the most trivial affairs of their lives, it is to be expected that this undue prominence thus given will single them out for censure as well as praise. Los Angeles is proud to be the motion picture capital of the world. While my acquain-tance with the men and women engaged in this industry is not large, I am persuaded* (the politician's "hedge") *that there are hundreds of clean, law-abiding men and women engaged in the making of motion pictures. On their behalf, I ask the open-minded judgment and even-minded justice characteristic of our American people."*

But, it was the words of Adolph Zukor which, upon his arrival in Los Angeles, drew the most attention. Famous Players-Lasky seemed to be the spawning grounds for almost all of Hollywood's torrid headlines these past several months—the Massachusetts scandal, the Arbuckle affair, and now the Taylor slaying—and the sentiments of that powerful corporation's president had long been anticipated: "*The one great remedial measure that will work a correction of the moral standards of our profession lies in the appointment of a vigilance com-mittee that will provide a safeguard for the good names of its members. Moral preachments, good example, and the charitable actions of many may have their good effects, but there must be something of more potent force than these to reach the minority. I am here to see that those few who violate the edicts of good conduct and bring discredit and embar-rassment to the many are ruled not only against, but out of the ranks.*"

The movie makers were no longer denying that there might be drugs and questionable moral values circulating within their indus-try, not that they were admitting it either; but if that were the case, then they were serving notice that they would stand against those who carried out these practices, providing it didn't damage their pocketbooks too much.

Detectives arrested one Walter Thiele on suspicion of burglary and, in searching the rooms he shared on West Fourth Street with L.D. "Red" Dailey, discovered a bloodstained cap, similar in type to the one mentioned by Mrs. MacLean as gracing the head of her "strang-er." Grasping at straws, police issued an all-points-bulletin for the man in connection with the burglary charge, but at the same time, made it clear to reporters that, once apprehended, Dailey would be grilled with regard to the Taylor slaying also.

We got some good copy out of this aspect of the investigation. Then, a few days later when Dailey was taken into custody, he cleared himself rather easily of any involvement in the murder case.

Producer Mack Sennett, who some gossips theorized might be jealous of Taylor because of his relationship with Mabel Normand, was finally questioned at his studio by a private detective hired by the industry brass, Charles A. Jones, former chief of police. On the night of the murder, Sennett had been with Thomas Ince and Al Lichtman to discuss distribution for the comedienne's new film, *Molly O.* The comedy giant talked freely with the investigator and offered to be interrogated at any time they thought he could offer them information of value.

Woolwine and Doran also questioned Chaplin's favorite leading lady and Taylor's next-door neighbor, Edna Purviance, at length. She offered very little of value, stating that she'd returned home late the night of February 1st, after visiting her mother. Although she'd noted that Taylor's light was on, the actress did not knock at his door, but simply retired to her own bungalow.

Another actress and former fiancé of Taylor, Neva Gerber, confirmed earlier reports received by prosecutors that the director was probably the "easiest touch" in Hollywood. She'd been called into the D.A.'s office after it had been discovered that, early in January, Taylor had written her a check for $500, which had immediately been cashed.

Following her hour-long session with Woolwine, Miss Gerber elaborated to the press on her relationship with the late filmmaker. *"Although our engagement was ended about two years ago,"* she said, *"Mr. Taylor and I remained the best of friends and frequently saw each other. His increasing moodiness and my mother's unwillingness that I should marry a man so much older than I were contributing causes to the broken betrothal, but I feel sure that he did really love me and I was very fond of him.*

"The checks which Mr. Taylor gave me from time to time can all be easily explained. During our engagement, Mr. Taylor gave me an automobile as a Christmas present. The machine was not all paid for at one time, and in order to prevent gossips from misconstruing the spirit in

which the gift was made, Mr. Taylor simply made out the checks to me so I could pay for the car in my own name. Numerous other checks were for distributing charity to the poor. Many a time Mr. Taylor would say, 'Neva, I know a poor family in desperate need. There are hungry children crying for bread and it makes me unhappy to think about them. You go see them and buy them what they need.' Always, of course, he would give me a check to cover the amount I had expended in relieving the case, and it was the bigness of his heart that made him feel this way and those who knew him think nothing of his giving me the money like that.

"As to the last check given to me a short time before his death, that can be accounted for very simply. Mr. Taylor was always looking after my career and doing all he could to help me progress in the film world. He knew I was in temporary financial straits at that time and voluntarily sent me $500.

"When Mr. Taylor returned from one of his overseas trips two years ago, he was gloomier and more despondent than ever. He told me that his sister's husband had been killed in battle and that during a midnight attack on London by German airships dropping deadly bombs, his mother and little daughter had been killed. Of course, I thought this was enough to account for his sadness, but besides his depression, he also grew irritable and it was the irritability that made me feel it would be a mistake for us to be married."

Miss Gerber's account was not without interest, but after doing a little checking, I couldn't help but wonder if the real reason why she and Taylor didn't marry was because, during their engagement, she was still married to Actor Arthur Nelson Millett.

14

About three-thirty Tuesday afternoon, I got a call from Willie Chang. I'd been writing up an exclusive interview that Sheriff William Traeger had granted me earlier in the day in which he'd discussed a narcotics ring two of his associates had been tracing that might possibly be linked to the Taylor case. Under sheriff Eugene Biscailus and Deputy Frank Dewar were on the trail of a "powerful group of peddlers," headed by a "beautiful woman" who lived in the vicinity of the Alvarado Street bungalow. The fact that since the murder, none of the gang had been observed in Los Angeles, had led investigators to wonder if there could be a connection.

Willie's accent was so thick it was difficult to understand what he was saying at times.

"Mr. Birnbaum," he said, "Mr. Grant asked me to call you. He said you wanted background on a story you're writing."

"That's right," I said. "When can we meet? Would it be possible for you to come up here to my office?" Dealing with underworld characters was rather new to me. I wasn't too sure how to play the conversation with my caller.

Willie, I know, was amused with my suggestion that we meet at the *Dispatch*, but since it would have seemed rude for a Chinese to exhibit this reaction, he patiently indicated the "proper" rendezvous point for the sort of meeting I had in mind, dinner tonight in Chinatown at a restaurant on Alameda Street called Tuey Far Low.

Immediately after I concluded my talk with Willie, I phoned Jerry Grant over at police headquarters to seek his advice on how to deal with my informant.

"You've got to remember he's a Chinaman," cautioned Jerry, "and even Chink stoolies conduct business in a prescribed manner. Make small talk with him until *he* brings up the reason you're there… which won't be until you've finished eating. To do otherwise would be impolite."

"What's Willie's racket?"

"I'm not positive, but I think he's a pimp; maybe he's into opium a bit, but not much.

"He's only half Chink though. His father was a sailor, who lived with his mother for only a few weeks. He deserted her when she got pregnant. Willie was about sixteen when she got killed—caught in the middle of one of those nutty Tong wars."

"Can I trust him?"

"Don't worry about that. I've always found him reliable, as long as he gets paid. Figure about twenty should do it. The one thing these guys are honorable about is their word."

I was excited, as well as a little apprehensive, about my meeting. It was a totally new experience for me, this journeying into the depths of Chinatown to have a clandestine encounter with an Oriental member of Los Angeles' criminal society. Not that I hadn't dealt with these types before. I'd interviewed many shady characters at police headquarters, the city jail, and the courthouse—but there'd always been cops and/or other reporters around. Tonight was to be my first solo into "enemy" territory and my stomach was playing the same kind of games it had that Saturday night when I was eighteen— the night I took out Sally Mundy, the neighborhood *nafka*, knowing full well I was going to get my first piece of ass.

Andy Lundy wasn't too enthusiastic about my plans—partially because he feared somewhat for my safety and, also, he didn't relish spending $20 on such a long shot. Nevertheless, I convinced him that we should, at least, get a good feature story about what devious dealings were going on in Chinatown that the tourist trade didn't know about and, if we were lucky, perhaps we'd get a fresh angle on the Taylor slaying, which we desperately needed.

If Carol knew where I was going, she'd have screamed her head off. So, since I could never lie to her—convincingly, that is—I asked Andy to call over to the studio and say that he'd sent me out on an assignment. When I got home, safe and sound (hopefully), then I could tell her where I'd been.

Chinatown of 1922 reeked with mystery. Its citizens, few of whom spoke English, seldom journeyed out of their self-contained community, which was centered around Alameda Street. People there seemed to be afraid of the Occidental, dealing with him as little as possible, although at restaurants like the Grandview Gardens, his dollars were quite welcome.

Most outsiders had heard stories about the opium and gambling dens that were supposedly hidden away in the bowels of Chinatown to cater almost exclusively to Orientals, as did also the houses of prostitution. Yet, if the Caucasian were willing to pay enough, he too would be allowed to sample these "forbidden" pleasures.

Then, there were the tales of the Tongs—the secret societies that battled each other within the boundaries of this city-within-a-city— and their hatchet men, who stalked the streets seeking their next victim.

A bit melodramatic, maybe, but for an outsider like myself, whose knowledge of Chinatown was based strictly on rumor, supplemented by an occasional fact, the place was certainly endowed with somewhat of a frightening atmosphere. Therefore, when I arrived at Tuey Far Low at precisely 8:30 P.M., I parked my car and proceeded double-time into the restaurant.

A hostess of gargantuan proportions ushered me into a private booth near the rear of the dimly lit establishment where a rather handsome Oriental, dressed in coolie coat and Occidental trousers, was waiting.

"Mr. Birnbaum," he said, rising from his seat and bowing slightly, "so nice of you to come." The man, in his late thirties, was nothing like the seedy character I'd conjured up in my mind.

Returning his gesture, I slid in on the other side of the booth. "I'm not in Chinatown often," I remarked, surveying the room. "It's an intriguing place."

"You should come more. Food here very good,"

The mention of food put me into a cold sweat. How could I, a kosher Jew, be in a Chinese restaurant when the basis of this cuisine was pork? I didn't want to refuse to dine with my host because I knew that Orientals were sensitive people and easily insulted. Perhaps the best approach would be to level with the man.

"Mr. Chang, I have a slight problem."

His face remained expressionless, which didn't make my task of explanation any easier. "You see, Mr. Chang, I'm of the Hebrew faith and it's against my religion to eat much of the food served here."

"Oh, so sorry. Please forgive my mistake."

"No, that's all right," I interjected quickly. "You had no way of knowing." A solution came to me. "I'll just have some tea… munch on a few fortune cookies. It's no big thing, really, I had a late lunch."

Actually, I hadn't eaten since breakfast and was famished, but I couldn't afford to blow this interview. My suggestion seemed to placate Willie and he put in our order.

People who eat with chopsticks have always fascinated me since I could never understand why they don't utilize a more practical utensil like the fork. I tried to amuse myself by watching Willie's dexterity with those Oriental inventions as he devoured a plate full of pork chow mein and egg foo young while, at the same time, I attempted to enjoy my delicious meal of fortune cookies.

"You are interested in the Taylor murder," he said, as we sipped our after dinner tea.

"That and related subjects."

"If I help you with this matter, would you be so kind and generous to give me twenty dollars?"

I quickly produced the money, but he refused to accept it until he'd completed his end of the bargain.

Willie looked at me intently, "I think maybe Taylor was killed by an Oriental." He noted my double take and continued. "It is the Oriental way to lay out body of deceased after death—same way Taylor was found."

An interesting thought, but since Willie had nothing more concrete to offer on this theory than his own suspicions, I mentally placed it in my "circular filing cabinet."

"Mr. Chang," I began, changing the direction of the conversation, "the police seem to think that the motive for the killing might have something to do with either narcotics—possibly a dealer killed him for revenge—or blackmail—an extortionist got angry when Taylor refused to meet his demands.

"Now, there are persistent rumors that many of the picture folk are on drugs and often come down here to Chinatown to attend 'hop' parties. Can you enlighten me at all in this area?"

Willie seemed quite frank, "I believe these film people do come here to smoke opium. I have seen well-dressed Occidentals in dens, but since I do not attend movie show, I do not know who they are... except Taylor. I saw his picture in paper last week and I think he was here a few months ago, but he did not smoke. . just watch."

"How about some of the other people who come down here? Have you seen their pictures in the paper?"

He shook his head. "Maybe. I don't know them though."

"Do the drugs or drug pushers that circulate in Hollywood come from Chinatown?"

"No, we sell only to our people. No outsiders, except Occidentals at parties. Drugs in Hollywood not from here, but they come here on ship like opium."

I asked about gambling, prostitution and the other vices I'd heard about. Willie was candid, in a general way, about the seedier aspects of his community, carefully avoiding names of any actual people or places. After a half hour with him, I was sure that if a professional criminal had carried out Taylor's murder, Willie didn't know who it was.

I may have been getting a good feature on Chinatown, but the conversation was going nowhere on the Taylor story, so I decided to call it a night and started to pay Willie his money.

"You say blackmail may be the cause of the murder?" asked my informant as he accepted the cash.

"It's possible. Why?"

"I hear of an Occidental gang of blackmailers in Los Angeles that take money from rich people."

"When? Where?" Maybe I was going to get my money's worth after all.

"My friend who works in laundry tell me this. He delivers shirts and overheard men talking. They live on second floor of apartment building at North Broadway and College Street."

"Do you know who was being blackmailed?"

"He tell me, but I forget. Not interested in movie people."

I thanked him for his help and he graciously escorted me to my car, which was still where I'd parked it. We shook hands and bowed, parting "best of buddies." Willie said I could call on him anytime for help.

It struck me while driving out of Chinatown, that much of Willie Chang—the pigeon-English, the stereotyped Oriental mannerisms— was probably a masquerade. After all, he was only half Chinese and knew the Occidental ways well. Playing the subservient role must be quite profitable for him.

I hadn't the slightest idea what I was going to find over on College Street at ten forty-five at night. And, what was I going to do there? Go up to a blackmailer and ask for an interview? For that matter, what did a blackmailer look like?

To my way of thinking, blackmailers were the lowest form of vermin. They preyed on the fears—sometimes unfounded—of their victims, threatening to expose the "sins" of their pasts or, lacking something tangible, would often manufacture "skeletons," which they'd hold over the heads of their prey. True or false, it made no difference, since the citizens of the motion picture industry found it cheaper to pay the tariff rather than risk any sort of scandal.

There was only one apartment building at College and North Broadway. I parked my Ford directly in front of the entrance to the fifteen-year-old brick structure—in case I needed to make a quick getaway—then just sat there for a minute, trying to convince myself to do the intelligent thing and call Al Drebin to come over here and join me. Being somewhat of a coward, I decided that I'd risk losing the exclusivity of the story and ring for help.

I phoned Al from across the street at a greasy all night diner. He wasn't at home, so I decided to leave a message at police headquarters. I was surprised when the desk sergeant informed me Al was there working. He must have been on to something pretty hot to be there at such a late hour.

"Al," I began when he finally grabbed the phone, "I'm onto a 'big' one. Can you meet me? I'm at College and North Broadway."

His voice assumed an incredulous tone, "College and North Broadway! An apartment house?"

"That's right," I said, wondering how he knew.

"Ben-a-la, get the hell out of there," he shouted. "Now!"

I was a bit confused by his outburst. "Why? What's wrong?"

"We've got that place staked out. Arrests are going to be made there tonight."

I told Al that I couldn't leave; I wanted the story, and I'd stay out of the way. He, in turn, announced that he'd be there in twenty minutes and that I should stay put.

I walked slowly back to my car. For the life of me, I saw no signs of a stakeout. A young couple holding hands was walking along on the other side of the street, but they turned the corner and disappeared into the blackness that enveloped this usually quiet neighborhood. Possibly Al had been mistaken about the address. Deciding to risk his censure, I entered the building to just look around. I don't know why I did it—maybe a combination of curiosity and blind stupidity that, in this instance, might have proved fatal.

The steps to the second floor were at the far end of the sparsely furnished deserted lobby. I climbed them slowly, cautiously, listening for any sound that would justify me turning tail and retreating back to the safety of my car.

Upstairs, the hallway was without décor, lit by two naked overhead bulbs. As I walked down the corridor I knew I was being watched; yet there was no tangible proof to underscore that impression.

A door at the end of the narrow passage opened and a short, clean-shaven man attired in a dark suit, cap, and muffler stepped out. He glanced up at me as I walked toward him and immediately the expression on his face became one of panic. Drawing a pistol from his coat pocket, he shouted inside the apartment from which he'd emerged, "Bulls!" then pointed the weapon in my direction.

Screw the story! I made the quickest about-face in history and started running back the way I'd come, only to discover two other ominous figures standing in the shadows, blocking my path. I couldn't see their faces, but what they held in their hands was quite distinctive.

I heard the report behind me, just as I felt the slug race past my ear. Now the men in front of me started firing and I dove to the floor, cowering next to the wall.

It was unbelievable—the gunshots, shouting, people running by me. I was afraid to raise my head to see what was going on. Maybe if they didn't see my face they wouldn't shoot me. At the moment, I wished I'd stayed in the clothing business.

The firing stopped. There were voices… more rushing around… and, ultimately, I gathered the courage to raise my head.

The first thing I saw was the stern face of Police Detective Sergeant Cahill staring down at me. Never was I happier to see anyone in my life.

"Birnbaum," he said, "what the fuck are you doing here?"

15

Thank God for Al Drebin. He saved my bacon after my College Street fiasco. Of course, he wouldn't speak to me for the next few days, but if he hadn't interceded on my behalf, I'd have probably gone to jail. Not that I didn't deserve that fate, since my stupidity nearly blew a five-day police stakeout.

The cops had received their own tip that a gang of blackmailers, which they later learned was eight in number, had been preying on the weaknesses of several vulnerable personalities whose identities were never divulged to the press. Their current mark was a Los Angeles businessman, from whom they'd demanded $25,000. Surveillance had been ordered on the apartment building; the whole operation was kept secret from the press corps because it was feared that some eager reporter might break the story too soon and thereby gut the entire operation.

Concurrent with my unanticipated visit to the site, authorities planned to move in on the gang, having learned that all members were then gathered together. And, I'd gotten right in the middle of the action.

My two "ominous" figures were actually Detectives Cahill and Cato, forced to close in prematurely when they saw me approaching the gang member dressed in cap and muffler, who was exiting the room in which his companions were congregating. It would have been very bad public relations for a reporter, albeit a nosey one, to be accidentally shot during a police raid, so the officers had moved before the appointed time in order to protect me. Luckily, no officers were injured, but it was perfectly understandable why I was in the doghouse.

The ironic aspect of this operation was that, after hours of grilling at police headquarters, it was announced that none of the blackmailers were involved in the Taylor slaying.

Further data about the director's early years came to light about this time—through the recollections of some of his former acquaintances. From Cappoquin, Ireland, Jim Cross, an elderly coachman once employed by the Taylor clan, reflected that the dead man's stern father had expelled him from his home when he failed an Army test. Taylor had been one of four children—two older sisters and one brother, Dennis, who was the father's favorite.

H.M. Horkheimer, a motion picture pioneer and former head of Balboa Film Corporation where Taylor directed his first film, related a rather unusual tale to the New Orleans press in which he claimed that Taylor had been murdered by a blackmailer who'd pursued him to America from Ireland. According to the retired producer, the slain director had confided this story to him when the pair had worked together at the now-defunct Long Beach studio. *"Taylor came from a fine old Irish family,"* he said, *"having entry in some of the best homes in England and Ireland. As a young man, he was engaged to a young girl from one of the most aristocratic families in the community. The prospective sister-in-law of Taylor was married to a man much older than herself and their marriage could hardly be called a love match. The young married woman was fond of gambling and often lost heavily at cards.*

"Unfortunately, there was among the society set of which she was a member what Taylor termed a 'parasite.' To this man she had become heavily indebted, and she'd given him checks on various occasions to discharge her gambling obligations.

"When she was unable to meet later obligations, the young woman conceived a plan of robbing the safe in her own home, and by stealing the money and valuables of her husband, secure enough to pay her debts. She planned to rob him on a night when a big affair was being

held and a number of guests were present. When the guests had retired for the night, it being a weekend party, the young married woman took a pistol from her desk and quietly stole down the stairs to the library where the safe was located. She'd opened the strongbox and removed a large sum of money when she was startled by a noise behind her. Turning, she came face-to-face with William Desmond Taylor. He ignored the weapon she brandished, stepped forward, and took the money from her. Then in low tones, explained the meaning of the terrible thing she was doing.

"Lurking in the shadows of the big library—unobserved –was the gambler. Swiftly the fiend laid his plans. Rushing from his hiding place, he deliberately upset furniture and created so much confusion that the other occupants of the house were aroused. Guests and servants immediately poured into the library. The lights were flashed on, revealing a strange scene. Near the safe, holding the money and bonds in his hands, was Taylor. Beside him, scantily dressed in a boudoir robe, was the wife of the host.

"In a dramatic voice, the gambler accused Taylor of robbing the safe. The husband of the woman asked his wife to explain her presence in the room. Blanched and trembling, she told a story of having heard a noise in the library, taking the revolver, and rushing downstairs to investigate. She said she found Taylor there before the open safe, the money and securities in his hands. Taylor, gallant to the last, glanced at the woman who accused him and at her beautiful sister to whom he was engaged. He chose to remain silent. His refusal to refute the charges of the gambler was considered an admission of guilt. Police were notified and he was taken to jail.

"Taylor was tried, convicted of robbery, and sentenced to three years in prison. After his release, he came to America and relocated in New York. Close on his heels was the gambler. For twenty years, the man instrumental in sending him to prison, the man who held the key to the closet that housed the family 'skeletons,' bled him for more money under threats of exposure of his past. It may have been the fear of this man and the weapon he held over his head that drove Taylor from New York to hide himself in another part of the country under an assumed name.

"It has been rumored that Sands, the missing valet of the murdered man, was related to him. This is not true. Whether Sands knew the secret of Taylor's past or whether he was the man the director feared remains to be seen.

"My theory is that he had decided to stop paying the blackmailer who had haunted his life, and that his refusal to pay more money to this leach resulted in the firing of the shot that killed him."

Rather an interesting, if melodramatic story from Mr. Horkheimer. Indeed, a few days later, it was discovered that the saga closely paralleled the plotline of one of Taylor's earliest writing assignments, *The Judge's Wife* featuring Neva Gerber.

Advised informally to avoid police headquarters for a few days, I sought out one of the very few people involved in the case who hadn't been interviewed in depth, as yet, by the papers.

Henry Peavey, the houseman, was back working at Taylor's bungalow—the police and Public Administrator having finished their duties on the premises—packing up his late employer's belongings for their ultimate disposal. He was a tall Negro, hesitant to speak with me at first, but amenable when offered a small gratuity.

There was an immediate response to my inquiry about Mabel Normand. "You can't tell me that Mr. Taylor wasn't in love with Miss Normand," he said. "Many's the time I saw him sit down in his living room, light a cigarette, and take up a book and begin to read, but he couldn't do it. He'd get up again and take down one of Miss Normand's photographs from the wall, lean it up against a jar or somethin' on the table, and just sit there smokin' and lookin' at the picture. Then he'd try to read some more, but he couldn't keep it up. He'd have to stop and look at the picture again.

"A while ago, Miss Normand was in the east an' every night I'd have to go an' send her telegrams. I never knew what the messages said because I can't read. Even if I could read 'em, I wouldn't of 'cause that wouldn't of been right. But every blessed night as I was about to call it a day, Mr. Taylor would sit himself down an' write her a telegram.

"Well, to come to her bein' here the night before the terrible tragedy. The day before Tuesday I made a custard and left it in the icebox. When I left Tuesday night, it had not been touched, but on Wednesday morning I noticed the pan was in the sink and all the custard gone. Well, on Wednesday—the day of the murder—I met Miss Normand and she told me that she had eaten practically all my custard. She called it puddin', but it was a custard and I knew what she meant. That's how I know she was at the house Tuesday night after I'd gone home. I don't know what she was doin' there and Mr. Taylor never mentioned that she'd been there."

And, Mabel had claimed that she hadn't been at the bungalow for months prior to the murder.

Peavey went on to describe another incident involving the actress at the Taylor residence. "Miss Normand came over one night and, after lookin' around, picked up a pair of scissors, pulled down three or four of her pictures from the wall, and sat right down on the floor. She began to cut up her pictures in small bits. Mr. Taylor noticed her and said, 'What's the idea?' She answered, 'I guess I can cut up my own pictures if I want to, can't I?' and he said he guessed she could. I don't know why she cut up her pictures, but I suppose she had some reason. Anyhow, if she'd been angry with Mr. Taylor at that time, they seem to have made up again later because I saw him on another occasion take her in his arms and she put her arms around him and they kissed each other."

According to Peavey, Taylor's attitude toward Mary Miles Minter was quite different from his feelings about the screen comedienne. He recalled that the young girl had come to the bungalow only once that he knew of since he began working there a few months back. She telephoned frequently, however Taylor would refuse to accept calls from her. Eventually, Miss Minter would not even ask to speak to the director, but simply inquire to see how he was getting along.

I felt sorry for Henry. He appeared to be a harmless sort, indecent exposure incident at Westlake Park aside. The good job and home he'd found with Bill Taylor had ended and where he would find new employment was anybody's guess.

There were others who did not share my benevolent opinion of the houseman. Redheaded and spunky Florabel Muir, Los Angeles correspondent for the New York *Daily News*, had confided to some of her fellow reporters one afternoon at the Press Club (I wasn't present, but heard the story later from Jerry Grant) that she was convinced it had been Peavey who'd straightened out Taylor's corpse before he summoned help.

About ten days after the slaying, she, along with her managing editor, Frank Carson, and Chicago-born circulation manager, Al Weinshank, "abducted" Peavey from his home one night, planning to scare a confession of murder out of him. Believing the old cliché that all Negroes feared ghosts, they took Henry out to the cemetery where the director was interred. Weinshank slipped away into the darkness and threw a sheet over his head, while the other two members of the fourth estate guided the Negro to the crypt.

Suddenly, the circulation manager leaped in front of the group and accused Henry, "I am the ghost of William Desmond Taylor. You murdered me. Confess, Peavey!"

It was a ludicrous scene. Peavey's eyes widened and he started to roar—not with fright, but laughter.

The conspirators, all of whom had probably had more than a few drinks, had forgotten one small item. William Desmond Taylor spoke with a clipped British accent, but Weinshank's words sounded like those of a Chicago hoodlum. The ploy may not have garnered the newspaper people a confession, but they certainly had a good laugh along with Peavey.

Authorities paid more serious attention to Peavey's possibilities as a suspect after they'd received a tip from one George F. Arto, a moving picture machinist, who said he saw the houseman and Mabel Normand's chauffeur talking with a third man in front of the Alvarado Terrace Apartments on the night of the murder. Driver William Davis denied this, swearing that only he and Peavey had been chatting together, the Negro having stopped on his way home. Their conversation was brief, and a few minutes after Peavey departed, Miss Normand, escorted by Taylor, returned to her car.

Neighbors reported the houseman had another Negro in the bungalow a few days before the killing. Questioned again, Peavey admitted that he *had* spoken to a colored friend named Anderson at the home. Henry had known the man several years before in St. Louis, and had met him by chance on Alvarado Street in mid-January. He'd taken Anderson to the bungalow while he had phoned an acquaintance regarding a possible job for the newcomer. Failing to garner results, they parted and Peavey hadn't seen the man since. Further inquiries into the matter failed to turn up any substantial leads, and investigators turned their attention to other areas.

Rumors, conjecture, shreds of fact; we of the press began to slap headlines on anything that would keep the nearly exhausted murder story on the front page a day or two longer. Chicago police were seeking Sands; Mabel Normand had moved into a new house and was on the verge of a nervous breakdown; film producers announced that they were beginning a program of self-censorship to prove that state boards were unnecessary; and Mr. Doran of the D.A.'s office had announced that, prior to his death, Taylor had received a threatening letter from somebody he'd called a "slacker" during the World War.

Doran also offered a possible, if ridiculous, explanation as to how the corpse came to be found in its unusual state: "*Such a position of the body need excite no comment as being an unusual phenomenon. The opinions we have secured are to the effect that a man in his dying paroxysms might throw himself into such a position. That there was such a struggle was indicated by the fact that his hands were clenched.*"

Little of this "news" was actually worthy of its placement in the nation's papers, and none of it was aiding investigators in accomplishing their ultimate task of apprehending the killer of William Desmond Taylor.

Then, on February 16, the world finally received word from "Edward Sands." Our resourceful District Attorney, Thomas Lee Woolwine, had made it clear by the press statements issued through W.C. Doran that, as far as he was concerned, the credibility of evidence amassed against the missing valet was suspect and a plea was made for

Sands to come forth and clear himself of the murder charge. The letter that arrived at the prosecutor's office that Thursday morning read as follows.

Mr. Woolwine
Los Angeles, California

Dear Sir:
    This letter will probably surprise you when you read it. I am taking the liberty to write you to make matters easier for you in the first place. I am Mr. Sands, although a friend of mine is writing this letter under my dictation.
    Mr. Woolwine, you need not look all over the world for me, for I am living right here in Los Angeles and am reading the papers every day concentrating on the Taylor murder. I will be frank with you, Mr. Woolwine. I haven't had any peace of mind since the murder and have come to the conclusion that the quicker this thing is settled the better off we will all be. Now, Mr. Woolwine, in the first place, I did not murder Taylor, but I know who did it. But what assurance have I from you to know that you will accept my story? None. Therefore, I want a guarantee from you that if I surrender myself into your hands and if I can establish my innocence of the crime, you will set me free. If you will do this, Mr. Woolwine, I can untangle this murder mystery for you. You might answer me in any of the Los Angeles papers.
    Thank you.

    E.P. Sands

Woolwine did not know for sure if the letter was a hoax or genuine, although he suspected that the former was the case. Proceeding, however, on the other assumption, he weighed the question of offering Sands immunity on the burglary/forgery charges. His answer ran in the major Los Angeles papers on Saturday, February 18.

"I am in receipt of a letter dated February 14, 1922, post-marked Los Angeles, which by its language purports to have been dictated by you (Sands). I have no present means of knowing whether or not the letter is genuine, as I have received vast numbers of bogus communications.

"The letter states as follows: 'I did not murder Taylor, but I know who did it,' and inquires in substance that if you come forward and surrender yourself and establish your innocence of this crime whether or not, I will set you free. The letter further states, 'If you will do this, Mr. Woolwine, I can untangle this murder mystery for you. You may answer me in any of the Los Angeles papers.'

"In answer to this communication, I wish to say that if Edward F. Sands will surrender himself to any police authorities or to me and establish to my satisfaction his innocence, and give information as to who committed this crime and untangle this murder mystery to my satisfaction as District Attorney of Los Angeles County, I will move for dismissal of the case of embezzlement now pending against him and set him free.

> *Thomas Lee Woolwine*
> *District Attorney*
> *Los Angeles County"*

We waited for the valet to reply.

16

Police headquarters wasn't the only place where poor Ben Birnbaum was drawing negative vibrations. When my wife learned what happened at College Street, I really "got it" at home.

"Jerk!" I was greeted with when I walked through the door Thursday night. "You could have been killed!"

What she was telling me I already knew, so it didn't make much of an impression. Indeed, I was so shaken by my harrowing experience of two nights before that, after being released by the police, I'd driven to a speakeasy and proceeded to get drunk. Carol had been asleep when I'd arrived home after three in the morning and, the following night, I avoided her questions about my "assignment."

"So who told you?" I asked, not bothering to deny her statement.

"I heard it at the studio. One of the girls there dates a deputy sheriff."

"Fine," I replied, in one of my acid tones. "I really don't need to get Hell from you, too."

She wasn't to be put off. "What would I do if you got killed?" she screamed.

"Okay… okay…."

"Don't you ever consider me when you do these things?"

"What 'these things?'" I countered. "I've never done one of these things before and believe me, I won't again. I don't have the nerve."

She stared at me for a moment, tears welling up in her eyes, and then she started to giggle. "You know something, Ben?"

"What's that?"

"You're sort of a *schmuck*." She laughed and I had to join her.

"I think you're right," I replied.

Later over dinner, she brought the Taylor case back into the conversation, "I wish you covered sports, or the stock market; anything but this sordid thing you're on."

In reality, I'd begun to think that way myself, but I remained silent while she verbalized her feelings.

"I realize," she said, "that you're covering a murder case and that the guilty party has to be caught. But, do innocent people have to be dragged down into the mud as a result? Look what's happened to poor Mabel Normand. She's on the verge of a collapse over the way her name's been tossed about in the papers. And, Mary Minter. God knows what the scandal will do to her career."

"Sometimes that sort of thing can't be avoided," was my feeble response.

"Maybe. But, tell me something, Ben—*honestly*," she was throwing down the gauntlet. "When you come home at night after writing one of those nasty stories, how do you feel? Do you feel good?"

I couldn't answer her question, or perhaps I didn't want to.

First thing Friday morning, I found a way to get back into the good graces of Al Drebin. A message was waiting for me upon my arrival at work from Sam Cooper of the Yellow Cab Company. Evidently, he had another "hot" tip and hopefully it would pan out better than the Meister one. I went right over to his office.

According to Sam, one of his drivers, a young man named Danny O'Shea, had not been seen since February 1st, the day of the murder. Even his wife didn't know his whereabouts.

The transportation supervisor hadn't thought too much about the disappearance since many of his drivers would quit without notice, although none, except O'Shea, had departed without picking up their final week's salary (in this instance, $14).

Then, on February 10th, the cabbie had shown up while Cooper was at lunch and claimed his wages from the cashier. This morning, O'Shea's wife, an attractive brunette, paid Sam a visit. She was distraught that her man was in some sort of trouble. While going through their rooms, the twenty-seven-year-old woman had discovered that a .38 caliber revolver, which had been hidden there for months, was missing.

Pondering the situation, Sam recalled that O'Shea almost always wore a cap and muffler. He then checked his files, noting that, within the past three months, O'Shea had answered calls at 404 S. Alvarado. Perhaps he'd driven Taylor at some point when the director was without his own chauffeur. In any event, Sam didn't believe in coincidence, so he immediately summoned me.

After speaking with the wife, I had to agree that Sam was right in being suspicious. I was about to leave with the woman for her apartment when I decided that maybe I should bring Drebin in on this one. After College Street, I owed it to him.

Al met Mrs. O'Shea and me outside her apartment on 17th Street and together we went inside for the purpose of searching the modestly furnished rooms. As a seasoned police veteran, Al was expert at going over a place in pursuit of clues and it wasn't long before he signaled me to come over and view what he'd uncovered in the dresser. Under O'Shea's socks were three .38 caliber steel-nosed cartridges—the same obsolete type of bullet that had killed Taylor.

Had we finally found our man?

17

One thing we weren't without the week of February 20 was new leads. An all-points-bulletin was put out on Dan O'Shea. There was no way of knowing if the taxi driver was actually the killer of Bill Taylor, but the man definitely had a considerable amount of explaining to do regarding his revolver, the bullets found in his room, and, most importantly, his whereabouts the night of the 1st.

While this action was going down in Los Angeles, Detroit authorities stumbled across an equally viable possibility regarding the case's solution. Henry Fields, a known drug pusher and pickpocket, had been arrested in that city and was telling his interrogators that he had, in fact, been paid $1,000 to chauffeur the killers of the director to and from the murder site.

Fields' story was akin to one of the rumors circulating around the Lasky lot that had, subsequently, been reported to the press. The informant claimed the shooter was a certain narcotics dealer who had been viciously beaten by Taylor because he insisted on selling his illicit wares to a film actress friend of the director. Fearing that Taylor would endanger his drug traffic, the peddler decided to avenge himself and, together with the addicted actress, carried out the crime. Although the star had no actual hand in the murder itself, Fields stated she signaled the shooting by waving a bag off candy.

Dubious as they were about Fields' tale, L.A. County Sheriff's deputies decided it might be worth further study after they learned from a local bank teller that, on the day following the murder, a man changed a $1,000 bill at his window, conducting himself in a "very mysterious manner." Photographs of Fields were requested from Detroit to see if the bank employee could identify the man.

Strengthening the theory that dope racketeers were responsible for the slaying was another startling revelation. Tom Green, an assistant United States attorney, announced that more than a year before his death Taylor had come to him to report the activities of a nefarious drug ring in Hollywood. The director was particularly incensed over the fact that the gang was selling upwards of $2,000 worth of narcotics a week to one prominent actress. He urged Green to use his influence to see that federal authorities undertake a war on narcotics in the show business community.

"So, what does this do to the other theories?" I asked Drebin when he told me about the Green disclosure. "Is Sands off-the-hook?"

Al stirred his coffee while he chose his words. "Let's say it depends upon which 'camp' at headquarters you belong to."

He noted my quizzical look and continued. "Some of us, as you know, have questioned the Sands angle all along. I have no idea if that letter Woolwine got was from the valet or not. Maybe we'll never find out. But, the point is that there's enough other evidence—circumstantial or what-have-you—floating around to make me, at least, seriously doubt whether Sands is anything more than a thief on the run."

"And what does the other half think?"

"Christ, guys like Jesse Winn wouldn't forget about Sands if you showed them a photograph of William S. Hart actually pulling the trigger. The Green statement had Winn stumped for maybe twenty minutes. Then, he came back with the idea that either Sands was a contact man for the peddlers or, at the very least, was blackmailing Taylor by threatening to expose him to the ring as the 'squealer' who'd been talking to the Feds."

"The actress that was mentioned—Mabel Normand?"

"Good guess, but prove it. I'll tell you something you didn't know. According to a couple of people close to him, Taylor was supposed to have spent nearly $50,000 of his own money fighting the drug racket."

"How the hell did he do that?" I asked.

"Beats me," admitted Al. "Green's been a little vague on that point, but he did say that Taylor supplied him with the names of several pushers operating in the area."

"Maybe he was buying information?" I offered.

"I must tell you this," Al chuckled as we departed the sandwich shop, "but forget where you heard it because, frankly, it's embarrassing."

"Who goofed up this time?"

"Not important. How long has it been since the murder, now? Three weeks or so?"

"Something like that."

"Yesterday, we got a 'brilliant' idea. Somebody remembered that Taylor's watch had stopped at 7:21 and suggested that this might be a clue of some sort. *Three weeks* later we think of this.

"So, we all get very excited, figuring that if the fall of the body stopped the watch, then we got a whole new ballgame, right? Taylor, then, would have been shot much earlier than we thought.

"Cato and I rush to a jeweler to see what stopped the watch...."

I had to beat him to the punch line, "And the jeweler said that the watch had just run down."

Al seemed disappointed. "How'd you know that?"

"Simple. If it'd been broken, you'd have told me about the watch first thing when we sat down."

Another possible solution to the case came to light when a Mrs. John Rupp of 1836 West Washington Street blew the whistle on a couple of her "good friends" who just happened to be members of a Los Angeles bootlegging gang that had quarreled with the film director. Taylor, evidently, had refused to pay the men for a particular shipment of "bonded" liquor, claiming that the merchandise was not as promised. When the mobsters objected, he threatened to blackball them with his other Hollywood friends who usually purchased the outlawed refreshments.

Why Mrs. Rupp sang was never made quite clear, although Al, who wasn't actually handling the arrest himself, thought the woman had a domestic argument with one of the men—Ray Lynch, her boy-friend—and figured that this might be an ideal way to get even, as well as collecting the several thousand dollars of reward money being offered by the Director's Association, Famous Players, the *Examiner*, and Mabel Normand.

Whereas six men were actually arrested thanks to Mrs. Rupp's tip, none were ever charged with the crime since all had airtight alibis. Nevertheless, two of the men were subsequently booked for stealing automobile radiators.

Too bad for the lady they weren't giving any rewards on that charge.

Just as suddenly as they appeared, the other new "solutions" to the mystery began to dissipate themselves. The bank teller, who'd cashed the $1,000 bill, was unable to identify a photo of Henry Fields and investigators ceased giving the story from Detroit further credence.

Locally, Danny O'Shea, after reading in the papers he was being sought for questioning, surrendered himself and, within a few short hours, had adequately accounted for his movements on the evening of the 1st. In addition, ballistics proved that his .38 was not the death gun.

Regarding the obsolete bullets found in his room, the cab driver claimed that a passenger in his vehicle had left them some weeks be-fore the murder. These facts certainly disappointed the homicide cops who had theorized that O'Shea might have been a hired assassin.

Then came the "confession" from Connecticut.

No well-publicized murder would be complete without its mul-tiple confessions. A certain kind of mind—publicity seeking and/or one wishing to inflict self-punishment for real or imagined "sins"—thrives on this sort of sensationalism. Within the first five weeks of the investigation, the Taylor murder had garnered a record three hundred of these false testimonies. They arrived in person and by let-ter from all over the country and, indeed, the world—from London to Buenos Aries.

Most of them were quickly filed under "crackpot" when it be-came obvious that the confessor knew nothing whatever about the true facts of the case. Some of these uninformed individuals had obviously not even read the newspaper accounts since they swore that they'd stabbed or clubbed the director to death and, in one instance, poison was the reported instrument of murder.

But the letter that Captain Adams received at month's end was different. Postmarked from a small town in Connecticut and bearing the obviously forged signature of a well-known Hollywood personality, the ten page account, written on hotel stationery, included small details about the crime, which caused police to seriously examine the correspondence in an attempt to identify and locate its author. The authorities weren't really convinced the author was the guilty party, but they were curious to know how he came by some of the little reported information.

"The only reason that I am writing this letter is that I want to help in clearing up this mystery," the anonymous communication read in part. *"It's not right to suspect the many persons who have been questioned in connection with the case, particularly the actresses who were on friendly terms with Taylor. For this reason, I want you to know that I am the one who killed Taylor; who shot him to death in his home; and I am not sorry that I did it; and as much as I'd like to see you get the reward for solving the mystery, I'm afraid you'll never collect. The reason is that my wife and I are on our way and I will never be arrested."*

Taylor, according to the letter, had been on very friendly terms with the wife of the writer, but *"he did not treat her right."* Finally, when the director told the woman that all was over between them she went straight to her husband and made a full confession of the sordid affair.

"It was then that I saw red," the man wrote. *"We both decided that he deserved to die and we planned to kill him."*

Driving to a spot near the Taylor home on February 1st at about seven o'clock, the couple waited for nearly a half hour, getting the lay of the land. They saw Henry Peavey come out of the court and talk for a while with Davis, Mabel Normand's chauffeur. Once, a woman passed them. She looked at them suspiciously, slowing down her gait to inspect them.

When Taylor and Mabel emerged from the court, standing by her car to converse for a few moments, the wife of the letter writer sprang quietly from her vehicle, entered the court, and slipped through the open door of Taylor's bungalow. The husband drove the car around to Maryland Street, then walked the short distance to the rear of the director's home. His wife admitted him through the back door and they went into the dining room where he concealed himself behind a drape.

Taylor re-entered the house and crossed over to his desk. He did not see the woman standing in the shadow of the door, nor did he see the signal she gave her husband. "Hello, William," she said.

The director turned. Surprised, startled perhaps to see her there, he started toward her but never made it. The husband had entered. "Stop!" he commanded, as he fired the single shot.

The couple moved quickly now. Not wanting neighbors to see two people leave the bungalow after the pistol shot, the woman left the house via the rear door, which her husband locked behind her. Then the man wound his muffler around his throat closely, pulled his grey cap down to his brows, hunched his shoulders to conceal his true height, and walked calmly out the front door, pausing momentarily on the porch.

He noted a woman (Mrs. MacLean) watching him through her window, so the killer turned back toward the door, opened the screen as if to bid a final good night to the man within, and then departed. Quickly, he strode to his automobile, which his wife had already started, and the pair drove off into the night.

One point that intrigued police with the letter was the correlation between the fact that the husband had entered the house through the rear and the earlier report from the MacLean's maid, in which she reported that prior to hearing the shot she'd heard somebody running in the service alley.

Working against the confession's credibility was the knowledge that all of the details included in the account had, in one form or another, been reported by the press. True, some of the facts had been passed over very quickly, but it would be possible for a person wishing to spend the time and energy on such a project, to manufacture this letter from newspaper stories alone. In any event, further investigation was warranted and, as a starting point, Adams submitted the letter to a department handwriting expert to see if it matched any of the samples of Edward Sands' scrawlings that were on file. It didn't.

With a revered evangelist like Billy Sunday making public statements about the murder, it's no wonder that the leaders of the Hollywood community were setting up their defense perimeters. The minister had been lunching at the White House with President Harding in a brief stopover on his way to Charleston, West Virginia, for a moral clean-up when he commented to the press: "*I believe that jealousy caused the death of William Desmond Taylor and, as a rule, there is always a woman in the background of such tragedies.*"

If jealousy was, in fact, the motive for the slaying, then of course it's a reasonable bet that a woman was involved somewhere. But what business of Billy Sunday's was it to comment to the press on the case? He knew nothing more about it than what had been printed in the newspapers and his theories were no more valid than my own rabbi's, who *hadn't* said a word about the story—publicly or in private.

"The Fight for Life" is what the movie people called their gathering that took place early in March, under the direction of industry leader Joseph M. Schenck. So important was the meeting for the show of industry unity, that production was stopped on forty-two features filming at the studios in order for it to take place.

The official statement issued at the session's conclusion read: "*We do not ask for special favors, but only the American principle upon which this democracy was founded, one of fair play. The recent unsavory publicity that has followed in the wake of the demise of the late William D. Taylor has resulted in the industry being maligned, mere rumor being accepted as fact, and idle gossip magnified into reality. Billy Taylor needs no eulogy. The life he led was but an indication of the true character of the man who was struck down by an assassin's bullet.*

"*The police have given to the public a theory that revenge accentuated the crime that resulted in William Taylor's death, exonerating the motion picture industry of any of its persona being implicated.*

"*We are not rampant with vice. The American public didn't attack all governors because a charge was filed against a certain state executive. Happy marriages far exceed those of divorce. Our church-going population is equally as much as those in other professions. Let him without sin cast the first stone.*"

Among the paper's signers were Schenck, Chaplin, Col. William Selig, E.B.P. Schulberg, Colleen Moore, Anita Stewart, Ben Turpin, Louis B. Mayer, Mack Sennett, King Vidor, Buster Keaton, Douglas MacLean, Marshall Neilan, and just about anybody else of any importance in the picture business.

Supplementing this plea was a resolution passed by the Los Angeles City Council requesting the public not to form hasty opinions of reported immoral activities of film people until definite facts had been substituted for the allegations.

In the meantime, Mabel Normand's health was failing fast, a severe case of influenza having struck her following her nervous collapse. Doctors feared for the comedienne's life.

"I think we should cut back on our coverage of the Taylor case," was the way my illustrious editor opened the conversation over the dinner he was treating me to at Cy's Downtown Delicatessen. Andy almost never invited a staff member out to eat—especially at a kosher restaurant. I, therefore, began to feel like the condemned prisoner about to partake of his last meal, since I knew that his forthcoming announcement would probably give me heartburn.

Noting my bland expression, he went on to explain, "The *Times* took the story off their front page two weeks ago; now, even the *Examiner* is losing interest in the thing. Circulation has dropped during the past week. Frankly, I think the story's tired.

"I know you've had something new to report almost every day, but we both realize that, with the exception of Tom Green's announcement, there's been nothing *really important*, happening for quite some time now."

"Well, the drug angle is certainly worth pursuing," I said.

"Of course, it is," he agreed. "But, not on a full time basis. I need you for other assignments. Grant is at police headquarters. If a 'hot' item breaks, I promise you'll get to cover it. The story will remain your exclusive domain. That's a guarantee."

Though unsolved, the Taylor murder had, indeed, become old news, so I really couldn't argue with Andy too much. Finding solid evidence to prove the narcotics angle viable was going to take time. Leads about pushers were hard to come by and everybody already knew that the picture folk weren't going to cooperate. All the trails being pursued now were leading absolutely nowhere.

"It's my feeling," Andy continued, sipping his matzoh ball soup, "that from the standpoint of libel, we're moving into a very dangerous area right now. That's another reason why I want to retreat for the time being. All we need is to print that some dumb bull said he thinks Mabel Normand is an addict and we're facing a lawsuit."

"Andy," I said, "this may come as a surprise, but I'm actually sort of glad to get away from the thing for a while. I'm too wrapped-up in it. It's becoming too strong an influence on my life. I've been ignoring my wife to work late and, hell, I've never done anything like what I did over on College Street. That was madness on my part."

"All right, it's settled. Tomorrow you go back to other assignments. When you start on Taylor again, it'll be with a whole new perspective."

The discussion switched to general shoptalk for the next few minutes while I savored my free meal and Andy tried to enjoy his, but some people simply don't have a taste for kosher food.

"You got a gut feeling about this case as far as who did it?" he asked.

"Not so much who," I replied, "but I'd bet my last dollar that the answer is hidden within the film colony—either in the relationship of some of its members to the narcotics pushers or, if not that, then the jealousy motive. I know that Eyton, or Mrs. MacLean, or *somebody* in Hollywood knows what really happened."

The death certificate for Manley Earl Tiffany, age twenty-nine, was dated February 26, 1922. The former chauffeur of William Desmond Taylor had succumbed at home to pneumonia. No autopsy was performed, as the physician in attendance confirmed the diagnosis via the clinical signs of the illness.

But, that made no difference. The police had lost their best witness against Edward Sands.

18

It was good to get back to writing mundane stories: city council meetings, bank robberies, and the occasional run-of-the-mill mass murder. Covering these events seldom required much time or effort, since the government body could only pass, defeat, or table a resolution, and when it came to crime, police usually had identified, if not apprehended, the culprit by the time the press corps arrived on the scene.

For me, life became simpler. Carol and I saw much more of each other and, around the middle of March, I achieved my goal. We made our first and only child. Carol balked when she discovered her family condition, as she'd wanted to wait a bit longer before taking that step. (I'd talked her into seeing Valentino in *The Sheik* for the third time, knowing that watching the Latin lover would put her in a most romantic mood.) However, within a few weeks, she eagerly anticipated the prospect of motherhood.

With the exception of an occasional small item, the Taylor case slipped off the front pages—even in the *Examiner*. The homicide sections of both the L.A.P.D. and the County Sheriff, faced with fresh murders occurring daily, cut their investigators on the case down to a skeleton crew. They knew the trail had become cold and some new turn-of-events would have to take place before a solution to the mystery was likely to develop.

Unfortunately, this disappearance of news about the case did not benefit the picture industry since on March 13, the third "Fatty" Ar-

buckle trial began in San Francisco and the world was, once again, reminded of Hollywood's "sins." The hearing lasted exactly one month,
but it took the jury a mere six minutes to reach their verdict—Not
guilty! Said the jury: "*Acquittal is not enough for Roscoe Arbuckle. We
feel a great injustice has been done to him and there is not the slightest
proof to connect him in any way with the commission of any crime.*"

The comedian's legal dilemma had ended, but not his ordeal.

Mary Miles Minter, accompanied by her mother and grandmother
(Julia Miles), arrived in San Francisco about the middle of March to
board the *Wilhelmina*, which was sailing for the Orient. The local press
got the tip, besieging the star in her stateroom. Finally, she unlocked
the door and agreed to make a brief statement. She said that notoriety
given her through the William Desmond Taylor murder mystery had
so shattered her nerves that she was forced to seek change and try to
forget. Her plan was to tour the Orient, then return for a stay in Louisiana (Mrs. Miles' home) before returning to picture work.

Interestingly, after an ominous beginning, the actress' newest
picture, *Tillie*, was doing an impressive box-office. In fact, next to
Anne of Green Gables, it was to become her most popular film. This,
as well as her next vehicle, *The Heart Specialist*, had been completed
prior to Taylor's death and it was speculated around town that both
projects fared well because of the public's morbid curiosity to view
one of those mentioned prominently in the well-publicized murder
case. Mabel Normand's *Molly O* happily endured a like fate for the
same reason.

It was, I believe, March 18 when Al Drebin called me at the office to
see if I wanted to take a drive with him to Mexico—to meet the "murderer" of William Desmond Taylor.

"About ten days ago," he explained, "this rancher out near Santa
Ana called us and said that, just prior to Taylor's murder, he was on
his way home from Bakersfield when he'd picked up these two rough-
looking hitchhikers. They said they were going to Los Angeles, then

to Mexico. In the course of conversation, one of the men told him that they'd served during the war in the Canadian Army under a captain named Bill."

"Taylor?" I asked.

"He didn't say and the rancher was too nervous about them being in his truck to ask any pointed questions.

"This 'Captain Bill' lived in Los Angeles and, since one of the men claimed that he was responsible for his being 'sent up,' they were out to get him. The rancher dropped the men in town here, but not before he noticed that one of them—named Spike—was carrying a .38."

"I'm sure there are a lot of captains in the Canadian Army named 'Bill,'" I said, not very impressed with what my friend had told me.

"Don't brush it off so quickly," said Al. "There's more. We got a letter about a month ago from this former British Army officer who told us that he'd had dinner in a London hotel with Taylor. While they were eating, a Canadian soldier walked across the dining hall and Taylor said something like, 'There goes a man who is going to get me if it takes a thousand years to do it.' It seems that old Bill had this guy court-martialed for stealing Army property."

"Coincidence," I said.

"Maybe, but the description in the Englishman's letter matches the one given by this rancher of Spike."

"Why did the rancher wait so long to contact you?" I asked.

"He says he doesn't see that many papers and only made the connection a couple of weeks ago.

"We put out an A.P.B. on these two characters and contacted the Mexican authorities. Yesterday, we got word from Mexicali that a Walter Kirby had been arrested in a bar there. He was wearing the same kind of cap as Mrs. MacLean described and when they went through his room, the Mexican police found Army riding breeches and leggings—several .38 caliber bullets."

"How do you know it's the same guy?"

"Number one, *schmuck*, he admitted to having served in the Canadian Army under Taylor; and two, a photo was sent up to Santa Ana for the rancher to identify—which he just did! Convinced?"

Mexicali is located just south of Calexico in the Imperial Valley. Like most border towns, it was wide open, attracting a good share of tourists and undesirables. I didn't really relish making the long drive over dusty bumpy roads, but if this new arrest signaled the final chapter in the Taylor murder, then I wanted to be in on it,

Getting the go-ahead from Lundy to accompany Al and another officer on their southern mission to bring back the suspect was a lot easier than garnering Carol's approval. Nevertheless, once I'd convinced her that the man was already in custody, that there was no danger, providing I didn't drink the water, and that after this trip it looked like the case would be closed, she bestowed upon me her blessing.

Officer Carlos Ramirez was the other cop making the jaunt down to Mexicali with us. A quiet, over-sized patrolman who worked on and around Alvarado Street, he was chosen for this plainclothes assignment because it was likely we would need the services of somebody who spoke Spanish. Ramirez drove while Al and I relaxed in the back seat of the unmarked police car—snoozing, when Al wasn't telling me his problems with the case.

Police were having virtually no luck at all coming up with material leads linking drug pushers to the killing. The only name they did have—Loper, the dealer Taylor was supposed to have beaten up on the Lasky lot—had dropped from sight.

"Have you noticed," Al said, "that Woolwine's office has backed away from the case?"

I had become vaguely aware that, following a few days of thorough reexamination of the witnesses and some statements to the press from Doran, the district attorney had, indeed, seemed to, lose interest in the mystery.

"Maybe he decided it wasn't going to be that easy to solve, after all," I suggested. "With elections just over the horizon, he can't afford to get involved in something where he and his staff aren't likely to come out the heroes."

Al lit up his stogie. "I know it's all political... *maybe*. But, Woolwine, Doran, and Asa Keyes are good, honest prosecutors. I can't believe they'd drop the thing only for the sake of the election. Even their investigators like Ed King are paying only lip service these days, almost as if they know something that we don't and they don't want to be bothered with long shot leads anymore. When they get a tip that looks interesting, they turn it over to us for follow-up. Hell, that Santa Ana rancher came to the D.A.'s office first. If they were still actively investigating the case, wouldn't they have run that lead down themselves?"

"What's your point?" I asked.

"I wish I had one. Christ, if the D.A. would let us poor, lowly cops see some testimony they're keeping under wraps…."

"What are they holding back?"

"Mrs. MacLean's *complete* statement for one thing."

"We keep coming back to her, don't we?" I observed.

"And they've been clamming up on that Sands letter, too—if it was, in fact, from Sands."

"You don't think it was?"

"I don't know. But if Woolwine's heard again from the valet, he's keeping it to himself. There's constant speculation around the department on that letter. Most of the guys think that either Sands chickened out and decided to skip, or that somebody from the studios got to him and paid him to disappear."

"I could buy that," I said. "As long as Sands is a fugitive and doesn't clear himself, the studios have their perfect scapegoat."

"We even got a call from a guy who said he was some sort of a psychic or fortune teller. According to him, he had this vision where he saw Sands being murdered by three gunmen, then they buried his body out toward Malibu."

"Did he say who hired the gunmen?" I chuckled.

"He certainly did. It was a studio boss who Sands phoned after he'd written the letter. He told the macher that he'd leave town if the studio would make it worth his while."

"So," I said, "the chief figured he'd save some bucks and, at the same time, give the police a fugitive they could never catch up with. Right?"

Al nodded. "You know, if that story had come from anybody except one of those 'hocus-pocus' guys, I think I might believe it.

"I just hope this trip to Mexicali ends the case. I'm sick of it."

We arrived in the squalid border town, thriving with panhandlers, street peddlers with their junk merchandise, and fat women begging coins for their starving babies, shortly after six and drove straight to the headquarters of the local constabulary. Colonel Jose Francisco Avila, a graying, but ruggedly handsome, bearded official whose gaze never left the eyes of the person to whom he was speaking, greeted us warmly and we immediately adjourned to a nearby cantina for some dinner. I, however, explained my dietary restrictions and ate a sandwich I had brought from home.

The Colonel was rather pleased that a newspaperman had accompanied the police to his country and, in reviewing the details of his easily executed arrest of Kirby for the benefit of his American colleagues, he seemed to direct most of his dialogue in my direction. He also made sure that I was aware of the correct spelling of his name.

"I am afraid, Senor Drebin, that you may have a problem with this man Kirby," announced our host, as we sat in his office later, waiting for the prisoner to be brought up from his cell.

"He hasn't reneged on waving extradition, has he?" asked Al.

The Mexican smiled. "Not in the least. This Kirby has been in jails on both sides of the border, and he says he much prefers the ones in the United States.

"No, he claims to have witnesses who can prove he was with them on the night of the Taylor murder. I know you will want to verify this, but I must admit, his story sounds very convincing."

Two brutish policemen escorted glassy-eyed Walter Kirby, a sullen, emaciated man of thirty, into the room. Al, who'd been quite friendly with Avila, suddenly turned businesslike. "You don't look too well, Kirby," he said. "The beer disagrees with you?"

"I'm fine," was the reply.

"We got a lot of questions to ask," Al said. "I hope you got the right answers."

"I didn't kill Taylor and I can prove it. That's all you need to know."

"We'll go over that in detail later. Now, you've caused Colonel Avila enough trouble, so I'll just take you officially into my custody and we can head back to Los Angeles."

Officer Ramirez, who'd been sitting quietly in a corner chair, grimaced at the thought of reversing his just completed long drive without getting some rest. Noting his reaction, Al said, "Don't worry, Carlos. I'll drive."

Drebin signed the necessary papers for the prisoner to be released to him and, after thanking the Colonel, we returned to the car.

It was insane driving back to Los Angeles at night, but all of us were anxious to give this viable suspect the acid test to see if his arrest had signaled the end of a seven week international murder investigation. True, Al could have interrogated Kirby in Mexico, but the witnesses who would ultimately confirm or deny his guilt—the Santa Ana rancher and Faith Cole MacLean—were in the "City of Angels" and any further time spent south of the border would only delay the mandatory confrontation.

Ramirez sat with the handcuffed prisoner in the back of the car while Al drove across the border with me in the seat beside him. Nobody said much. I was tired, taking the opportunity to catnap. Al trained his full attention on the blackness of the road ahead.

Just north of San Diego, I awoke, suddenly becoming aware that the vehicle had stopped. Al had pulled off the highway to relax for a few minutes.

"I'm going to stretch my legs," he said, motioning for me to stay put. Then, he turned his attention toward Kirby, "Walk with me, Walter. Let's get acquainted." The prisoner hesitated. "Don't worry, fella. I'm not going to hurt you."

Al took Kirby by the arm and together they faded up the highway into the night. Evidently, he'd decided not to wait until we'd returned home to start his questioning. While Ramirez dozed in the back, I stepped out of the car and leaned against the hood, straining to distinguish what my two traveling companions were saying. It was useless. There was the mumble of angry voices several yards away from me, then the sound of cloth ripping, a thud and moan. Shortly thereafter, Al and his limping suspect emerged from the darkness and I noted that Kirby's shirt had been torn.

"The bum's an addict," announced Al, pushing the man back into the automobile. "There're needle marks on his arm."

"What about Taylor?" I asked.

"Says he didn't do it."

Driving the rest of the way back to town, I thought about Al. We'd been close for years, yet I'd never known him to rough up a prisoner before. Not that I was so naïve I wasn't aware that this was rather common police interrogation procedure, but Al had always seemed to be above such violent behavior.

Twenty-four hours later, Kirby, who'd refused to speak with me or any other reporters, was a free man. Upon our return to Los Angeles, Al assigned a man to check out the prisoner's alibi. The rancher from Santa Ana was called in for a show up, but to everyone's surprise, was unable to identify Kirby as the man he'd picked up. As he told me later, "The hitchhiker was many years younger and much shorter than the man under arrest here."

Kirby admitted to the police that he had served under Taylor during the war, but was not out to "get" him. He did not own a revolver and had found the .38 shells two weeks previous in a San Diego hotel room.

Al had planned to ask Mrs. MacLean down to headquarters when word came back regarding Kirby's alibi. It checked. The man had been working as a dishwasher in a Los Angeles restaurant when the murder took place and he had half a dozen witnesses who could testify to the fact.

That did it. Since no drugs were found on him, Kirby was released before any reporters could interview him, and he immediately skipped town. The Taylor case was no closer to being solved than when it began.

I went back on general assignment again—covering all sorts of uninspiring items, although I did sit in on the Madalynne Obenchain murder trial when the regular reporter came down with influenza. In fact, I was there near the end of March when the jury came back in to announce that they were deadlocked. The judge declared a mistrial and the new hearing was set to begin on June 5.

The next few weeks provided a constant, if futile, surge of activity surrounding the Taylor case. Plenty of leads were popping up around the country, sending our hometown cops scurrying about in a frenzy. Predictably, none of them seemed to pan out.

The department's chief supporter of the Sands theory, Sergeant J.A. Winn, journeyed to San Francisco to interview a former L.A. newspaperman who was known to carry a revolver and also, on the night of the murder, had stopped in a steam bath frequented by drug addicts. The trip was a total waste of taxpayers' money.

In New York City, one Anthony "Scarface" Gessell, a drug dealer, claimed that he'd personally sold narcotics to an actress prominently mentioned in the case and that a Los Angels drug ring had killed the director because he attempted to impede their business. A few miles away from that metropolis in Poughkeepsie, police were holding drug addict F.A. Doran (no relation to our deputy D.A.) on a Chicago murder warrant and were theorizing that he might also be tied in with the Los Angeles case.

Another dispatch from the East Coast claimed that the highly touted Connecticut confession letter had actually been mailed from Atlantic City, New Jersey. However, *who* had written it was still unknown.

It was the beginning of May. Working the news desk, I'd been taking a story from Jerry Grant who'd called in the facts about an arrest of a Chinaman—Henry Lee—in a North Flower rooming house. The armed man was being held on the state poison act, having been found with ample supplies of both cocaine and opium in his possession.

We were about to terminate the call when Jerry was interrupted by one of his colleagues in the police pressroom. Thirty seconds later he was back on the line, "You remember that guy from Mexicali—Walter Kirby?"

"What about him?" I asked.

"They just found his body."

19

Two small boys rabbit hunting in the swamp bottoms of New River, located west of Calexico in the Imperial Valley, discovered Walter Kirby's partially decomposed remains. Speculation was rampant as to the cause of the addict's death. A Mexicali informant claimed that, shortly before Kirby had vanished from the border town, he'd mentioned that someone was after him and would "end him quick."

Toxicology detection methods in 1922 were not as refined and sensitive as they are today, so nobody was ever quite sure if Kirby died of a drug overdose, exposure, or starvation—or perhaps he was killed by a means known only to the border underworld. In any event, most Los Angeles investigators quickly laid his death to coincidence and, within a couple of days, the incident was virtually forgotten.

It was "crackpot time" again—at least as far as the police and press were concerned—when a dispatch was received from Laramie, Wyoming, which told of a William *Edward* Taylor, who claimed to be the son of the late director. The young Taylor was on his way to Los Angeles to attempt to prove his relationship and also to seek a share of the $25,000 estate left by the dead man to his daughter, Ethel Daisy Tanner.

William Edward was basing his assertion on records in an old family Bible, statements of a midwife and nurse, and what he said was his resemblance to the murdered man in a peculiar slant of the eyes. According to his statement, in 1886, the young man's mother, Olive Randall, married William Sinclair Taylor in Laramie. This fact was recorded in the Bible. William Sinclair and William Desmond Taylor, as per the testimony of a midwife and a nurse present at William Edward's birth, were one and the same.

The claimant did, in fact, arrive in Los Angeles. However, executors of the director's estate paid scant attention to his demands for recognition.

The Madalynne Obenchain murder case captured Los Angeles headlines again on June 5, when the accused woman's second trial was called into session. Lasting until the second day of August, this hearing ended like the first—the jury deadlocked.

Poor Tom Woolwine had spent months preparing and prosecuting this case. After the second trial of Arthur Burch, Mrs. Obenchain's alleged co-conspirator in the murder of Belton Kennedy also ended in a hung jury, the District Attorney realized that it was virtually hopeless to try to obtain convictions on the available evidence. So, by the end of the year, all charges against the pair were dismissed.

Whereas we of the Los Angeles "fourth estate" had our hands full covering more current news events than the Taylor case, the motion picture community was still under heavy fire from the out-of-town sheets and reform groups regarding the sensational disclosures that had been brought forth about the rampant use of drugs in Hollywood. It was time for Will Hays, President of the M.P.P.D.A., to start earning his $100,000 annual salary.

"The potentialities of motion pictures for moral influence and education are limitless," said the ex-Postmaster General. *"Therefore, its integrity should be protected as we protect the integrity of our children and our churches, and its quality developed as we develop the quality of our schools."*

Among the steps the Hayes Office instituted in its campaign to clean up the image of the film capital, was to devise the "morality clause," which posed the threat of contract cancellation over any performer involved in a scandal. The Central Casting Agency, through which extras were hired, was established so that prostitutes could be identified and banned from industry work.

Following the acquittal of "Fatty" Arbuckle, Hays, who'd ordered a national ban on the comedian's films during his trials, maintained a prudent silence for a few months, then made a public statement: "*Every man in the right way and in the right time is entitled to his chance to make good. It is apparent that Roscoe Arbuckle's conduct since his trouble merits that chance. So far as I am concerned, there will be no suggestion now that he should not have his opportunity to go back to work in his own profession.*"

The reform groups were incensed with Hays' suggestion. From pulpits throughout the land, priests, ministers, and rabbis alike denounced Arbuckle and the movie industry he was a part of. One do-gooder summed up the national attitude with: "*If society allows itself to be guided entirely by the Gospel rule, 'Let him who is without sin cast the first stone,' no one would ever be convicted of a crime. I do not believe in such ready forgiveness. Arbuckle is not the proper person to appear before the public. He has misbehaved and deserves punishment at the hands of the public.*"

For the final eleven years of his life, the fat funnyman was forced to pay the price of his indiscretions. Broke and unable to work in films, he attempted vaudeville and nightclubs, but embittered by his experiences, failed to garner laughs. Eventually, he was able to get work as a movie director, utilizing the pseudonym of William Goodrich.

Shortly before his death in 1933, Arbuckle was on his way to a minor comeback. He'd been signed by Warner Brothers to star in a series of comedy shorts to be shot in Astoria, Queens, New York. Two days after he'd finished the last of these pictures, "Fatty" succumbed in his sleep—the victim of a heart attack.

However, in 1922, Will Hays' biggest problem was to curb the threat of political censorship. When he assumed office, seven states had already provided for state censorship and, within the next few months, similar bills were introduced in thirty-two state legislatures. The greatest danger to his cause was an upcoming public vote in Massachusetts, since if political censorship prevailed in that state, it would surely sweep the entire country.

Hayes hired a number of speakers to tour the Bay State to educate the populace on the dangers of censorship. Responsible citizen committees also joined the crusade. Basically, the argument the M.P.P.D.A. president and his aides presented was that the only satisfactory way to protect the public interest without destroying or impairing the vitality of motion pictures was for the industry to control itself. The studios, since the Arbuckle and Taylor tragedies, had become well aware of these considerations and were making every effort to achieve the desired moral goals. The first of these steps was, of course, the formation of the Hays Office. In sum, the speakers argued, self-regulation should be given a chance to prove itself.

Massachusetts decided to give Hollywood that opportunity and, on November 10, 1922, the people of that state overwhelmingly rejected the censorship proposal. Hays had won his battle. With the exception of Louisiana and Connecticut, no other state enacted similar legislation.

Nevertheless, in the summer months of 1922, before any Hays victory was on the horizon, the studios were in quite a quandary regarding what actions to take to protect their interests. Writer Elinor Glyn, when asked by a *New York Times* reporter what would happen in Hollywood in the wake of the recent scandals, replied, "Whatever will bring in the most money will happen."

The British import wasn't wrong and one of the leaders in revitalizing the screen fare was none other than Cecil B. DeMille, whose boudoir-oriented films had received a goodly share of criticism from censorship groups. In 1923, the director made his moralistic spectacle, *The Ten Commandments*, and shortly thereafter, he produced another biblical epic, *King of Kings*. They, indeed, made a lot of money.

But it was the morals of the stars and their reported use of narcotics that were causing the greatest problems. Rumors of an upcoming secret "summit" meeting, at which time all the major studio executives would try to find an answer to the perilous question, began to circulate in late June.

Carol mentioned over dinner one evening that she'd learned of the possibility of such a conference from one of the other secretaries at Lasky. I, in turn, told Andy Lundy, who agreed with me that, should the rumor turn out to be fact, I should definitely get into that meeting. How—I didn't have the slightest idea.

"It's at the Beverly Hills Hotel," whispered Carol over the phone, "in about an hour."

My adrenalin started pumping at an increased rate. "You're sensational!" I beamed. "How did you find out?"

"I can only talk for a second," she said. "Both Mr. Lasky and Mr. Eyton just left for the hotel in separate cars. I overheard Eyton talking with Carl Laemmle of Universal this morning and he mentioned a two o'clock meeting. Why would everybody schlep way out there if they didn't want to keep a secret?"

Carol had a point. Built in 1912, the Beverly Hills Hotel was originally designed as a residential hotel for senior citizens. The expensive homes that populate the now high income community had not yet begun to spring up, nor was it to become the prestige transient home for the world's VIPs until years later. In fact, much of the acreage surrounding the lodge in 1922 was nothing but bean fields. It was a perfect rendezvous point for the studio executives to meet in private, away from eyes and ears of Hollywood gossips.

I told Andy of Carol's call and he gave me the go ahead, authorizing me to draw $30 from the cashier, should I need to bribe a hotel employee in order to gain access to the conference. As I departed, my editor said, "Any of that money you don't have to spend, you buy your wife a present—with my compliments. And, tell her thank you."

It took me better than a half hour to get to the Los Angeles suburb of Beverly Hills on that hot July day. I had no idea how I was going to accomplish my task when I arrived; however, upon turning up the driveway to the main entrance, I knew Carol had been correct. There, in the parking lot, were at least a dozen limousines with their chauffeurs standing around chatting among themselves. In 1922, only film people owned cars like these.

The attendant condescended to park my Ford and I entered the hotel's plush lobby. Who in this establishment would know where this summit meeting was taking place and, at the same time, be willing to aid me in my quest? The desk clerk? Not likely—he was too close to the management to betray a guest's confidence.

I spotted the restaurant off the main foyer and I had my answer—room service. Those underpaid waiters were always willing to earn some extra cash and my elusive executives were sure to order some kind of refreshment. I approached a middle-aged steward who appeared to be unoccupied at the moment.

"Yes, sir?" said the waiter, flashing a courteous smile.

I looked around to see if anyone was in earshot. "Would you be interested in earning a ten?"

"How may I be of service?"

"There was a meeting scheduled to start somewhere in the hotel about ten minutes ago. A dozen or so businessmen would be attending."

"They would probably be in a conference room, sir."

"I don't think so. It's a *secret* meeting and they're more than likely to be in a large suite. You handle room service calls, don't you?"

"Yes, sir."

"Well, when they call down, I want you to tell me where they're at, then either put me in the adjoining room or somewhere that I can overhear what they're saying. Can do?"

"You said twenty dollars, sir?"

"Fifteen. Take it or leave it."

I waited in the lobby while the waiter checked with the kitchen to see where my parties were and if they had indeed phoned for room service yet. It was two-twenty when he returned. "An order for a large pot of coffee was just called in from bungalow C out back," he said. "Fourteen cups were ordered."

"That sounds right," I said.

"About the only thing I could suggest, sir, would be for you to place yourself underneath the living room window. You won't be seen from the main building and, if I open the window when I bring the coffee, you should be able to hear fairly well."

That wasn't the ideal solution, but since it appeared to be the best I was going to get on such short notice, I handed my confederate his booty, which disappeared into one of his pockets before I had a chance to blink, then walked out to the hotel's patio area to await his emergence from the kitchen with the order.

I stayed about ten paces behind him, as he pushed his service cart along the carefully landscaped walk to bungalow C. Reaching the door, he motioned me to walk around the corner of the building, which I did.

The living room window was large and I immediately squatted down next to the wall beneath it, sinking my newly shined shoes into the mud of the freshly watered flowerbed. It was about a minute before the waiter earned his money and opened the window above my head. I had no idea as to who was inside that room since I dared not peek through the window, lest I be discovered, and the voices were not that intelligible.

They were talking about Arbuckle, Bill Taylor, and the national attack that had been unleashed on Hollywood morals. "What are we paying Will Hays for if not to take care of these problems?" piped in one voice.

Another executive said that the studios had to back Hays' promises of a moral clean up. Then he announced, "I've a list here of industry personnel that we've investigated during the past couple of months through a private agency. It's the opinion of the detectives that these individuals present a high moral risk...."

"Fire every one of them!" interjected an angry voice. "We'll blacklist them all from the studios."

"That might be a little difficult. Some of the people are in this room."

There was a pregnant pause. The next voice I thought I recognized as Eyton's. "You know," he said, one of the ironic things about this whole mess is that the person I've covered up the most for these past months was Bill Taylor."

A murmur of voices, as the other men in the room demanded an explanation.

"He may have presented a dignified image to everyone else," continued the studio manager, "but, as far as I'm concerned, he was one of the most ruthless bastards in this town.

"Ever wonder how he made it so big at Lasky so fast? How he got those choice assignments so early in his career? He blackmailed his way into them. Said if he didn't get what he wanted, he'd tell the press about all our actresses who visited his bungalow at night. He even threatened to blow the whistle on Wally Reid...."

The man with the list interrupted. "We should discuss Reid," he said. "His problem is getting a little out-of-hand. How much longer can it be hidden?"

"Look," said Eyton, "Reid's contract is worth two million. You want to drop *your* naughty players, we'll consider firing *him*."

An elderly couple walked around the corner of the bungalow, stopping in their tracks when they saw me. "What are you doing there?" demanded the man.

That was it. The executive had heard him. Startled, and realizing I had to make a quick exit; I lost my balance, sitting my *tuchis* right into the mud. Cursing the fact that I was going to have to have my suit cleaned, I scrambled to my feet and ran back to the main building, just as I heard the bungalow door open.

I was disappointed, but Andy was mad. Since I couldn't be positive as to exactly *who* was at that meeting, I had no story and everything I'd listened to was simply hearsay. If we'd printed it, the *Dispatch* would, most likely, face a libel suit.

Within a couple of weeks, however, it was obvious that nobody in the industry was going to be blacklisted. What studio would be willing to flush its most valued assets (i.e. its stars)—tainted or not?

Those who bought the theory that a dope dealer killed Taylor got some strong support in December. A burglar named John Marazino was apprehended as he tried to enter an apartment through the window. He was carrying a suitcase full of women's clothing.

Questioned by the police, the illiterate young man claimed he often dressed as a female to elude a professional triggerman named Jack Kramer—the "murderer" of William Desmond Taylor. Marazino said he'd met a drunken Kramer a few months before in a Denver bar, where the latter mentioned that he was "on the lam" because he'd killed a movie director—as ordered by a narcotics dealer named

Loper. Realizing that when he sobered up, Kramer would be after him, Marazino fled and had been hiding ever since.

Authorities started searching for Jack Kramer and, again, for Loper. However, they were unable to find a trace of either one.

Discussing the burglar's story with me later, Al Drebin expressed his reasons for placing a certain amount of credence in it. "Marizano can't read," he said. "So, how would he know the minor details of the case unless somebody told him about it?"

Yet, after a week or so of further investigation along those lines, police officially went back to the Sands theory. As Al explained, "Somebody's putting political pressure on somebody to drop the drug angle. We got the word from upstairs that we were to concentrate on finding Sands and *that's all*."

20

After Will Hays' Massachusetts' electoral victory in November of 1922, Hollywood began to breathe a little easier. The public, it appeared, was not about to "tar and feather" the entire community, but was, as requested by the M.P.P.D.A. president, willing to let the picture folks regulate themselves. With the Arbuckle scandal past history, and the Taylor case out of the papers for weeks at a time, even the studio executives seemed to be relaxing again.

On January 18, 1923, the newly found bliss was shattered. Death in the form of renal suppression and hypostatic pneumonia took the life of one of Hollywood's brightest stars. Normally, the passing of such a popular leading man during the prime of his life would elicit an outcry of anguished national mourning from the actor's fans, as well as his friends and business associates. But, in this instance, the demise rekindled in the studios the recently discarded fear of public sanctions. Wallace Reid's death had been brought on by *"nerve exhaustion due to withdrawal from morphine. Duration: three years."*

It wasn't long before the background of the tragedy was made public. Reid, the star of such pictures as *The Affairs of Anatol* and *Forever*, who possessed a rare innate personal charm, had become addicted to the drug in 1919, as the result of a head injury he'd received while on location in the Sierras. Blinding headaches forced physicians to give him pain-killing injections so he could continue acting. Reid was restricted to bed for three months after the picture had been completed and received regular doses of morphine. He was never able to withdraw from the drug. Actually, many soldiers wounded and hospitalized as a result of the war, suffered similar fates.

According to his widow, actress Dorothy Davenport, Reid did not feed his drug habit by going to underworld sources, but would "charm" doctors into giving him the tablets he needed. When, in November, the actor's dissipated condition could no longer be hidden from his friends or, more important, movie audiences, he decided to enter a sanitarium.

Mrs. Reid, in an effort to avoid the vicious gossip that attached itself to both the Taylor and Arbuckle affairs, called in the press to give an honest account of her husband's innocently contracted illness. Her straight forward approach worked and, although there was the expected negative reverberations from some reform groups, the more general reaction from both the public and industry leaders like Will Hays, Jesse Lasky, and Cecil B. DeMille, was to rally around the ailing star and offer moral support. The papers kept the public informed almost daily of Reid's involvement—to the point where everyone thought he would be returning to the screen at any moment. It was a shock to all of us when his condition ultimately weakened and he succumbed.

Luckily, for the nervous picture industry, people felt that Wallace Reid's losing fight against drugs had made him a martyr and the anticipated reborn cries for censorship—except from some diehard do-gooders—never took place.

Mary Miles Minter also left the Hollywood scene in 1923. Unlike Wally Reid, she didn't die, but her career certainly did.

She'd returned from her vacation in the Orient carrying more pounds than when she'd departed. Famous Players-Lasky wasn't sure what to do with their star, so they cast her in a half-dozen features, including *Drums of Fate* and *The Trail of the Lonesome Pine*. None of the projects fared particularly well at the box-office, so after Charlotte Shelby balked at her daughter being assigned to a western—*The Covered Wagon*—the studio reassessed the ingénue's value and decided to settle the balance of her contract. Mary also had been quarreling openly with her overbearing mother and this sort of negative publicity, coupled with her recent notoriety with the Taylor case, was also a factor in Lasky's ultimate decision to drop her.

Carol was no longer working at the studio when Miss Minter left just short of her twenty-first birthday. Our son, Joshua, had been born in January and she was enjoying her motherhood. One day she supplied me with a bit of inside information she'd neglected to tell me months before: "Remember when the *Examiner* and the other sensational papers were printing all those innuendoes about Mary and Bill Taylor? You know why Mrs. Shelby never sued them?"

"I'm in total suspense," I said.

"The studio wouldn't let her; said that the publicity would be disastrous coming so close to the Arbuckle mess."

"What good did it do her not to sue?" I observed. "They got rid of her anyway."

Although Mary Miles Minter was never to make another motion picture, she was to remain in the public eye for years to come.

There was one other departure of note during the first half of 1923. Because of a serious liver ailment, Thomas Lee Woolwine, the southern gentleman from Tennessee, resigned as District Attorney in June, to be succeeded by his deputy, Asa Keyes. A highly regarded public servant, Woolwine died in July of 1925—his loss lamented by all who knew him.

But what we didn't know in 1923, was that one of the prosecutor's last acts in office would definitively affect the outcome of the William Desmond Taylor murder case—well over a decade later.

21

The Teapot Dome Scandal, the Leopold/Loeb case, the Scopes "Monkey" trial and Al Capone's bloody activities in Chicago stole the nation's headlines for the next few years. On the Hollywood scene, Charlie Chaplin married sixteen-year-old Lita Grey, film pioneer Thomas Ince died under "mysterious" circumstances, and both Metro-Goldwyn-Mayer and Columbia Pictures were established. Movies themselves were getting a lot better. Lon Chaney in *The Hunchback of Notre Dame*, Buster Keaton in *Sherlock Junior*, Douglas Fairbanks as *The Thief of Bagdad*, Ramon Novarro as *Ben-Hur*, and other such entertainments kept audiences glued to their theater seats.

William Desmond Taylor? His murder became a popular topic of discussion at parties—when the more current news had exhausted itself. Sure, every six months or so some new story remotely tied in with the case would pop up somewhere. For example, in July of 1923, police in Martinez, California, arrested a man named Albert Sans, who was alleged to have been writing threatening letters to both Mabel Normand and Mack Sennett. After reading a number of these penciled notes, officials advanced the theory that Sans was suffering from a hallucination that he was the slayer of Taylor and that he believed himself Miss Normand's promised husband.

Less dramatic was Ada Deane-Tanner's courtroom appearance in 1924, to request that her long-missing husband, Dennis, be declared legally dead. Her petition was granted.

If the Taylor murder itself wasn't making sensational headlines, the problems of some of those involved in the case certainly were.

Unfortunately—or fortunately depending on your point-of-view—I observed most of these events from a distance. When our son was born, Carol and I reached an understanding. She agreed to give up working permanently and I, in turn, promised to adjust my work schedule as much as possible, to eliminate overtime, travel, and odd hours.

I was lucky. Andy Lundy had offered me a dual inside job about that time—assistant editor and my own column, "Inside L.A.," in which I would focus on unusual people and events in and around town. Although I found the position confining at first, I soon slipped into it rather comfortably, preferring to spend my off-hours as a husband and father, rather than playing journalistic sleuth.

A few weeks after Famous Players settled her contract (for a reported lump cash sum of $350,000), Mary Miles Minter turned twenty-one. Almost immediately, the actress moved out of her mother's mansion and Charlotte Shelby left for Europe.

On August 10, 1923, Mary hired attorney Neil McCarthy to institute a lawsuit against her mother for an accounting of the $1.5 million she'd earned during her last few years as an actress. It was her contention that Mrs. Shelby had taken charge of her money and dissipated it. In her filed brief, Mary made some interesting revelations:

"I was constantly repressed by my mother; my life was dominated by her, and this was caused in part by the fact that my mother was, herself, in love with William Desmond Taylor.

"Mother's actions over Mr. Taylor's attentions to me were not inspired by a desire to protect me from him. She was really trying to shove me into the background so she could monopolize his attentions and, if possible, his love.

"He used to call at our house, but as soon as Mother saw his preference for me, she put a stop to his visits. Until she found I loved him, she had only praise for him. Then she turned against him. Why? Because I found out she cared for him herself.

"I pleaded with her to let me see him, but she would not. He went to Europe once at the same time we did, but she would not let our paths cross. When we all returned to Hollywood, he was forbidden at the house."

It was at this point in time that Mary announced that she and Taylor had been engaged to be married.

Two Chicago reporters were able to obtain an interview with a maid in the Shelby/Minter household, who said, *"Mrs. Shelby had a pistol and did regular target practice in the basement of the house. She went to Taylor and threatened his life if he did not stop seeing Mary, especially if he did not stop her midnight visits to him."*

Police, searching the Shelby house, are said to have found bullet fragments—presumably from a .38—in its foundation. And, about that time, the new District Attorney, Asa Keyes, made a public statement about the case: *"The person wanted for this murder has fled the country."*

Obviously, Keyes' proclamation was politically motivated. If he'd had a reasonable case against Mrs. Shelby, assuming she was indeed the party he was talking about, then he would have certainly taken steps to bring her back from Europe. But, the D.A. didn't attempt extradition and, therefore, his public disclosure was quickly forgotten.

This was the first, but definitely not the last time the redheaded Mrs. Shelby's name was seriously mentioned as a possible suspect. Many more fascinating revelations were yet to come.

The suit, which was only the first of several public quarrels Mary Minter and her mother engaged in over the years, was finally settled in 1924, out of court for, according to insiders, $200,000.

Mary was in New York in 1925, when her grandmother, Mrs. Miles, died of cancer in Los Angeles. Although air "ace" Eddie Rickenbacker offered to fly her to the West Coast, weather prevented the plane from taking off and the kind old woman died without her favorite granddaughter present. Shortly thereafter, Mary journeyed to Paris for a reconciliation with her mother.

Mabel Normand's life following the Taylor mess was far more tragic than that of "the lonely princess." She recovered from her bout with influenza and went on to star in two more pictures for Mack Sennett—*Susanna* and *The Extra Girl*, as well as some shorts for Hal Roach. Things seemed to be going well for her until New Year's Eve, 1923.

Mabel, on that fateful day, was the guest of Edna Purviance at the actress' new home on North Vermont. Also attending the party was Denver oil millionaire Courtland S. Dines.

Into the festive gathering strode Horace Greer, Mabel's chauffeur (William Davis had long since been terminated) who, as was learned later, fostered a secret admiration and jealousy where his mistress was concerned. Producing a gun, the servant opened fire on Dines. The millionaire was badly wounded and Greer surrendered himself to the police—later being acquitted at his trial.

Dines recovered, but the publicity was the *coup de grace* for Mabel's screen career. It made no difference that she was really only an innocent bystander again. Self-appointed censors around the nation insisted that her movies be banned.

In 1924, she would suffer another nervous breakdown, complicated once more by influenza. Two years later, in September of 1926, she married fellow actor and longtime friend, Lew Cody. Those close to the couple later admitted that the marriage was actually the end result of a prank at one of Mabel's parties. Somewhat "loaded," Cody had proposed to the funny girl, and she, pretty much in the same condition, had accepted. With a group of friends, they drove up the coast to Ventura, where a justice-of-the-peace was awakened to perform the ceremony.

Yet, as the story goes, the union was never consummated. On the way back to town, both Mabel and Lew realized that they'd made a mistake, but instead of incurring the adverse publicity a divorce or annulment would bring, they decided to stay married in name only—separate residences were maintained.

Mabel was stricken with bronchi-pneumonia in February of 1927, and her health was never really good from that point on. When her ailment was definitely diagnosed as tuberculosis in September of

1929, she was removed to Pottenger's, a Monrovia sanitarium. She died on February 22, 1930, weighing a mere sixty-eight pounds.

Shortly before she succumbed, Mabel whispered, "I wonder who killed poor Bill Taylor."

It depressed me to learn of Mabel's death. Despite her personal problems since the Taylor murder, which had virtually marked the beginning of her descent, I'd remained a loyal devotee of her talent. She was one of a kind. Journalist Adela Rogers St. Johns, who knew her well, described her as "*a pixie… an elfish clown and, as we all know, it's impossible for an elf to live among mortals.*"

Was Mabel a drug addict? That's not an easy question, since none of the evidence presented on the point is conclusive. Some swear that she was, while others strongly dispute the claim. More certain is that she definitely enjoyed her liquor. In fact, those who insist she was on drugs say she was placed on narcotics by doctors in order to relieve her of her drinking problem, which is said to have approached alcoholic proportions. The cause of her thirst? Possibly the disastrous end to her relationship with the one true love of her life—Mack Sennett—in that darkened bedroom she'd entered unannounced.

In any event, via the yellow ink of the press, the world had been deprived of a very special human being. She'd been butchered—for the "public's right to know"—just like a steer in a slaughterhouse. I wondered, as I read Mabel's obituary on that gray morning, if things would have been different with her had I and my fellow journalists cared more about people—and not simply selling newspapers.

Back on the investigative front, events didn't start to get really intriguing again until mid-October of 1925. Rumors began fluttering through the air about then—all originating from the District Attorney's office—that new evidence had been discovered in the Taylor case and the mystery was on the verge of being solved.

I checked with Al Drebin on these stories, but he'd heard nothing—on or off the record—from his superiors, and was just as much in the dark as to their reliability as the press was. Sandy Haines, who at times assisted me in covering the initial weeks of the Taylor murder, was assigned to see what he could uncover around the prosecutor's office. Haines, incidentally, had become a fine reporter, specializing in securing confidential information from public officials and, after the *Dispatch* folded in 1933, he moved to Chicago to work on the *Sun*.

When D.A. Asa Keyes and his assistant journeyed to San Francisco that October, tales ran rampant that a new witness—one who was said to have seen the killer depart the Taylor bungalow—had been found. Partial verification of the report came when it was learned that Detective Ed King of the D.A.'s office and Jesse Winn from L.A.P.D. had again been working on the murder, having spent recent time checking through original investigative records.

Keyes put an end to the speculation when, from the Bay City, he expressed his indignation at the rumors: "*This is a terrible thing to get out. Nothing could be more inopportune if I were on the Taylor case, and whoever has given out the information will certainly get what is coming to them.*

"*No, I am not here in San Francisco on the Taylor matter. If I were, I couldn't admit it. Neither can I tell you why I am here. Just say it is in connection with the jewel thefts of 'Big Bill' O'Connor.*" (This master thief, who was in the San Quentin infirmary on his deathbed, had informed authorities that he was willing to disclose the hiding place of $100,000 worth of jewelry he'd stolen from the Provident Loan Association in Los Angeles.)

Despite Keyes' denials, rumors continued for months that the District Attorney was on to some new evidence that could, at any moment, provide the solution to the four-year-old mystery. Those who were "in the know" stated off the record that what was needed was the corroborating testimony of Edward Sands—the long missing valet—to finally end this most baffling case. Ergo, when, early in March, Keyes and an aide hastened to the East Coast, the L.A. papers once again returned William Desmond Taylor to their banners—declaring that the identity of the killer would soon be revealed.

From Boston, on March 20, 1926, the Associated Press "quoted" Keyes as saying that Mary Miles Minter was at Taylor's home a few hours before the murder. It was a revelation that raised a few eyebrows since Mary, in her 1922 statement, had claimed that she'd not been to the bungalow for some time preceding that day. Indeed, houseman Peavey reported the director had left word he was not to be at home to Miss Minter either when she telephoned or called in person.

Jaunts to New York City (to speak to Mabel Normand, who departed before he arrived), Syracuse, Philadelphia, Detroit, and various other eastern cities by the prosecutor brought further promise that an "important announcement" was forthcoming. Chief Deputy D.A. Burton Fitts, who was carrying on his own re-investigation in Los Angeles, was not denying these reports either.

Sandy Haines came back from the prosecutors' office one day during this period to present two rather interesting "new" facts. The first gave certain credence to the theory Willie Chang had expressed to me years ago in that Chinatown restaurant.

Investigators were working on information that a Chinese man who knew Taylor intimately killed him on behalf of a Spring Street narcotics ring. The director, it was said, had threatened to break up the dope ring and the Oriental was sent to the bungalow to kill Taylor quickly and quietly. The method of murder used, according to authorities, was Oriental—a single bullet and the body was laid out carefully.

The other revelation was reported by Detective King, who announced that "two strands of blonde hair were found on Taylor's body shortly after he was discovered murdered and safeguarded by the D.A.'s office since that time." The strands, from the point-of-view of the investigator, seemed to indicate that a woman may have either committed the murder or was present when the fatal shot was fired.

This, of course, was no news to me. With the understanding that I not print it, Al Drebin had told me this fact the day after the body was found.

Keyes, again, threw "cold water" on our hopes for a solution to the case when, on March 25, he wired Burton Fitts from Chicago to deny all statements attributed to him by the nation's press—including the one about Mary Miles Minter being in the Taylor bungalow just prior to the murder. He said, "My presence in Chicago was purely for the purpose of visiting the State's Attorney to see how he handles crimi-

nal cases and to make train connections. My travel has no connection whatsoever with the Taylor investigation and we were not shadowing two so-called 'hangers-on' of the Hollywood film colony in Chicago. The latest reports are absolutely false. In all fairness to her, Mabel Normand has long since been completely exonerated of any connection with the matter. The questions to be asked of her on my return are only of minor importance and of a general nature."

The career of Asa Keyes, considered by his peers to be a brilliant prosecutor, came to an unfortunate end. In 1928, he was defeated in a re-election bid by former deputy, Burton Fitts, who had since become California's Lieutenant Governor. A month later, Keyes was indicted on charges of receiving bribes in the Julian Petroleum conspiracy case. His successor both prosecuted him and obtained a conviction.

Near the end of 1929, former California Governor F.W. Richardson made a rather startling disclosure about the Taylor affair. The ex-chief executive let it be known that, three years earlier, he'd received "positive information" that a "certain top screen actress" had murdered the director. He was unable to do anything with his knowledge at the time, suggesting that much of the Los Angeles city and county governments had been corrupted by bribes from motion picture studios to "bury the investigation."

After a bit of intense questioning, Richardson admitted that his source of information was Otis Hefner, a Folsom Prison parolee, released at the then-governor's personal solicitation.

Without exception, Hefner's tale—that he'd been with Edward Sands on the night of the murder and together they'd seen the unnamed actress depart the bungalow after the shot was fired—was dismissed by investigators and reporters alike as having no real basis in fact.

Reached for comment at the county jail where he was awaiting action on his appeal from his bribery conviction, former D.A. Asa Keyes summed up the general reaction to the convict's claims: *"It is worth exactly nothing at all. Hefner has times and places all confused. His statement that he and Sands saw Taylor at Redondo Beach is absurd. So is his story about seeing a mysterious woman leaving Taylor's house. Taylor was dead before two o'clock that morning."*

What the Hefner/Richardson folly boiled down to was this: The convict had wanted out of prison and, in order to achieve that end, had played on the then-governor's gullibility to prove that there was, indeed, one born every minute.

Hefner wasn't the last person to falsely claim he had the solution to Taylor's murder. But, very shortly, new concrete disclosures from an unexpected source would permanently alter the course of *serious* investigation this bizarre case would take. The final act, albeit seven years in length, was about to begin.

22

Wall Street laid its mammoth egg on October 29, 1929. That Black Tuesday saw sixteen million shares dumped overboard on the New York Stock Exchange for whatever price could be obtained. Within minutes, millionaires were reduced to paupers; families saw their life savings wiped out; and many a stockbroker took a multi-story leap from the nearest office building.

A few short months later, unemployment had skyrocketed and the apple peddler became a familiar sight on every street corner.

At the *Dispatch*, all employees were given a salary cut; my $65 per week was slashed to $57. I didn't like it, but it was better than not working at all. How else was I going to support my wife and six-year-old son?

Shortly after the crash and almost concurrent with the disclosures from former Governor Richardson and ex-convict Otis Hefner, the ladies Minter and Shelby wormed their way back onto the front pages. Mother and daughter, seemingly reconciled from their previous legal battles, had been residing together in Paris, as well as other European cities, for a number of years. Mary's "valuable" golden curls were no more—bobbed into a chic Parisian headdress—and, she had put on weight.

In February of 1928, *Photoplay* had run an interview she'd granted in her rooms at an unostentatious hotel on a quiet street just off the fashionable Champs Elysees. In it, the actress, who'd once rivaled Mary Pickford, commented on her lost career and subsequent misfortunes: "*I haven't read a newspaper or magazine about myself since 1923. What's the use? One blunder, one mistake, one misfortune, and fame becomes infamy. The climb to public favor is sweet. The fall is swift. The return journey is interminable.*

"*But long ago, I was named as co-respondent in a divorce case. A man I had only met in a casual way. When the news reached me, I was in Italy with my mother. Investigation brought out the fact that the wife of the casual acquaintance had selected my name as being the most sensational one on which to base a divorce suit.*

"*I wanted to sue the wife who had taken recourse to such unfair methods in order to win her freedom, or whatever it was she hoped to win. My attorney advised me against the procedure.*

"'*Drop it,' he said. 'Your friends know better. Folks who like to believe such things will believe what they want anyway, no matter how much you exonerate yourself.'*

"*I took my attorney's advice. One blunder. One mistake. One misfortune. The fireworks forever after.*"

The women had returned to the United States in 1929 and, if Mary's "fireworks" had not been too apparent to us Angelinos before, the situation certainly changed just prior to Christmas of that year when Charlotte Shelby called in the press and made a quite surprising public announcement: "*The rumors and gossip that I killed Mr. Taylor to preserve my love and Mary's future, and that I was jealous of Mary are absurd.*

"*I am seeking definite information of the things said against me. I am going to take action to the limit of the law.*"

Since Mary's 1923 suit against her mother and the interview given the Chicago reporters by the Minter/Shelby maid, wags had indeed conjectured about the possibility of Mrs. Shelby being the director's killer. Clues like the blonde hairs found on the corpse and the elusive nightgown and undergarments, as well as both Mary's and the maid's statements, gave credence to possible motives. The woman either wanted to break-up her daughter's potentially career-damaging relationship with Taylor or was jealous that he was not showering his attentions on her.

Further support came from Faith Cole MacLean's admission that the person she saw emerging from the bungalow could have been a woman dressed as a man. Then, there were the bullet fragments in the cellar… but no gun.

On the other hand, Mrs. Shelby's movements the night of February 1st had been checked, and it was found that she had an "iron-clad" alibi. She'd been playing cards all evening with friends, among them actor Carl Stockdale, who'd appeared with Mary in films like *The Eyes of Julia Deep.*

Until she'd come forward, Charlotte Shelby's supposed guilt had, for all practical purposes, simply been a favorite topic of cocktail chatter. Police, if and when they still worked actively on the case, publicly supported the Sands theory and privately looked toward the narcotics trade for the enigma's solution. Had Mrs. Shelby made her statement years before in answer to Asa Keyes' assertion that "*the person wanted for this murder has fled the country,*" then one could understand why she'd want to defend herself. But, why remind the district attorney, police, and the press of an "ugly" story they'd long since dismissed?

"*I am a woman alone,*" she declared. "*I was not in love with William Desmond Taylor. I was not in love with anyone. And, no one was in love with me. I never held a purely social conversation with Mr. Taylor in my life. He was always aloof, a man of mystery, polished, distant, and removed.*

"*For years there have been malicious innuendoes and rumors against me. I did not kill William Desmond Taylor. I do not know who did kill him. I demand a complete exoneration or an indictment for murder.*"

She went on to deny that she'd ever threatened the director or that she'd purchased a revolver and practiced shooting with it a short time prior to the murder. Regarding her visit to Taylor's home, as reported by the maid, she said, "*One night Mary did not come home for dinner. I began to worry. We called up everybody she knew. We thought perhaps Mr. Taylor would know, but we did not have his telephone number. We started for his home, my secretary, my cameraman, and myself.*"

Taylor was at home, she said, and she asked if he had seen Mary. He hadn't. "*After some conversation in which I mentioned my fears of an accident,*" she continued, "*I left and went home.*

"Certainly this incident is not a hot murder clue. Had there been anything sinister about it, I would not have taken two witnesses with me. I know there have been reports I was in love with Mr. Taylor, that I was jealous of my daughter and feared that Mary's career would suffer, and that I killed Taylor to preserve my love and Mary's film career. I repeat these things to show the absurdity of them. Killing Mr. Taylor would have wrecked Mary's career instead of saving it."

One thing about Charlotte Shelby you had to admit: she sure as hell had a lot of *chutzpah*.

Again estranged from her mother, Mary Minter replied from her luxurious Pasadena apartment, *"I have absolutely nothing to say about the William Desmond Taylor case. I do not care what my mother has said. I am not interested."*

Nor did D.A. Burton Fitts care to discuss Mrs. Shelby's challenge, stating that he had dropped the case and would call neither Mrs. Shelby nor Miss Minter to his office for questioning. However, Superior Court Judge William C. Doran, formerly Thomas Lee Woolwine's Chief Deputy District Attorney, did grant an interview.

"The investigation of the murder of William Desmond Taylor developed no evidence in any way implicating Mabel Normand or Mary Miles Minter," he said. *"I interviewed all the persons in the Taylor case who could have known anything of importance about it. Their statements were all preserved in writing. Among those I questioned were Miss Normand, Miss Minter, and Mrs. Charlotte Shelby.*

"The evidence was so limited that if someone would come forward and confess the murder, he would have to produce corroborative testimony before his confession could be accepted. He would be compelled to substantiate his confession by other credible testimony in order to secure his own conviction. And that, in my opinion, would include even Edward Sands.

"The net result is that I believe to this day that the Taylor case belongs among the unsolved crime mysteries of the world and the chances are good that it will remain there."

Interesting that Judge Doran, despite the woman's then-current newspaper coverage, didn't specifically mention Charlotte Shelby for exoneration. A simple oversight or had the jurist chosen his words carefully?

Others involved with the original investigation began to make candid statements to the press. Ed King, Woolwine's chief investigator, said in 1930: "*We had never been satisfied that the person seen by Mrs. MacLean, emerging from the Taylor residence, was not a woman in disguise as a man. Almost from the first I have* known *who committed the murder. But knowing it and proving it are two separate things.*"

A few years later, the sleuth would make another, more revealing disclosure: "*We know, of course, who committed the murder. But, there is no evidence for the Grand Jury. The woman who killed him mentioned his murder to her chauffeur at seven o'clock in the morning, a full hour before Peavey found him lying dead; before anybody except the murderer herself knew that he was dead.*

"*We have had the woman in for detailed questioning, but she is a shrewd and cunning person, and refuses to talk to us.*"

Why hadn't King mentioned the woman by name? To do so without possessing the needed evidence would have been slander. He was too much the professional to commit that act.

Police Lieutenant Al Drebin had no idea who King was talking about in his statements, since the prosecutor's office did not care to confide this information to members of the L.A.P.D.

"You know, Ben-a-la," Al remarked one Sunday afternoon while he was giving my son, Joshua, a piggy-back ride across the living room floor, "I had a hunch eight years ago that King and Woolwine knew who killed Taylor. A week after they assumed control of the case, they clammed up on whatever results they were getting out of their investigation."

"As I recall," I replied, "Woolwine pretty much seemed to drop the case."

"It all makes sense now," Al said, starting back across the throw rug with Joshua digging his heels into his sides. "King was satisfied that he had the answer, but he couldn't prove it. So he and his friends decided to let us cops waste our time chasing the 'red herrings.' Back then, the D.A. couldn't very well announce he knew who the killer was without making a formal indictment. The public would've lynched him."

"So, who is it? Charlotte Shelby?"

"If she is, it's sure a surprise to me. We never found anything to tie her into the killings."

"What about her target practice in the basement?"

"So what? Nobody ever found a gun—and even if we had, what's so unusual about owning one? They're found in just about every household. Without a ballistics test, we got no case.

"No, I still think that some drug dealer, maybe even a woman, pulled the trigger, or, at least, paid to have it done."

23

Whenever a "forgotten" hot news story reappears in the nation's headlines, it's common practice for reporters to seek out the people involved to reminisce about the original event. Therefore, with Richardson/Hefner and Shelby/Minter gathering so much space, it was only natural for the *Dispatch* to go after the recollections of the other participants in the melodrama—like Henry Peavey.

Sandy Haines spent a couple of days trying to track down Taylor's former houseman, but all he could learn was that the man had moved to Sacramento several years before. Prior to the stock market crash, Andy Lundy would have thought nothing of sending a reporter north to the state capitol to get the human interest interview, but since that tragic day, the paper's operating budget just wouldn't allow it.

A week later, a stroke of fate altered the situation. An aunt of Carol's, who just happened to reside in Stockton less than fifty miles from Sacramento, died and the two of us took the train up to attend the funeral. The day following the rites, I borrowed her cousin's car and drove into the larger city to seek the ex-servant.

Finding Henry Peavey wasn't difficult. Within an hour of arriving in the ramshackle Negro section of the capitol, I found somebody who could direct me to the decaying rooming house in which he resided.

The man had changed considerably during the eight years since I'd last interviewed him. What was left of his hair was now snow white and his always slender frame protruded through the paper-thin flesh surrounding it. Although he didn't recall our previous meeting, he invited me into his cramped, dusty, one room flat, motioning me to sit across a table from him on a three-legged stool.

"I know all about Mr. Taylor," he said. "I worked for him when he were killed." It was obvious that Peavey enjoyed talking about the case. After all, his minor involvement in the matter was the one claim to fame in his otherwise mundane life.

"This picture actress... She shot him," he continued, seemingly in a mild trance. "She did it sure enough."

"What actress?" I asked. "Mabel Normand? Mary Miles Minter?"

"Oh, I don't remember their names. But, the paper said this here actress did it...."

Peavey's mind, never the sharpest mental instrument, appeared to have lost considerable ground over the years. "I remember... about a month or two after Mr. Taylor was killed... this man... he might have been a policeman or somethin'... He come to me and say, 'Boy, if you know what's good fer ya, you better leave Los Angeles.' He give me a hundred dollars and say that he didn't want me around in a week. So, I done got out."

We talked for about an hour. Henry didn't know who the man was who ordered him out of town or whether he was even an official. For the most part, he simply reiterated—quite sketchily—the same facts he'd told me and the authorities eight years earlier.

When we were finished, he saw me to the door and I stuck a couple of dollar bills into his shirt pocket, for which he thanked me. "You know, sir," he said as I stood out in the hallway, "this Mr. Taylor case gets on my nerves. My memory doesn't work too good when I have to think that far back."

A year later, in 1931, Henry Peavey died of general paresis in a mental hospital at Napa, California.

With the Taylor case in the news again, the "screwballs" returned in force.

A "confessor" named Rinaldo came forward and, after being questioned, was held for mental examination.

From the police department in Birmingham, Alabama, came an amazing description of the murder by a man who claimed to be an eyewitness to the shooting itself. According to this self-admitted racketeer, he'd entered the Taylor bungalow by mistake and was hiding behind the piano when a woman entered, had some brief, angry words with the director, then shot him.

Things were fairly quiet the day the "piano story" came over the wire, so even though nobody really took it seriously, we ran it on the *Dispatch's* front page.

On January 22, 1931, the grim reaper took another Hollywood luminary—actress Alma Rubens, age thirty-three. Although her death was directly attributed to lobar pneumonia, the world knew that the thing that had actually put her in such a weakened condition was her addiction to morphine.

In late 1932, Andy Lundy died in his sleep of heart failure. One of the "greats" of our profession, his passing was mourned by all who either knew him or had read his insightful editorials. Two hundred or more people attended his funeral, most of them members of the "fourth estate." I have missed Andy every day since his passing.

The *Dispatch* was never the same again. Our absentee owner/publisher, who ignored the operation of his concern because he preferred to spend his time in Europe, left the job of finding a replacement for Andy to the paper's prosaic controller, Ralph Edmunds.

Edmunds was very competent when it came to business matters, but he knew as much about the editorial aspects of newspapers as I know about brain surgery. Deciding that the publication should shed its conservative image for one of more sensational impact, he hired Donald Austin, Associate Editor of a New York tabloid, to take over the *Dispatch*.

Austin and I just didn't get along. He was a "yellow" journalist of the worst kind, caring little for the true facts of a major news story if they didn't contribute to a sensational headline. More than once during the week I worked under him, we did battle in this area. He wanted me to rewrite my copy to give a particular story a different slant, which would have conveyed to readers a dishonest picture of the events that actually took place. I'd refuse and he'd have the piece rewritten to be printed sans my byline.

The coarse son-of-a-bitch was also a Jew-hater. After a few days of constant fights on editorial matters, he threw the word "kike" into the conversation. Thirty seconds later, I was unemployed and he had a broken nose.

I was only out of work for two days. Once it was learned that the writer of "Inside L.A.," by then the town's most popular column, was available, offers came in from both the *Times* and the *Examiner*. But, I went to work for a local radio station—KRP—to serve as their on-the-air reporter/commentator twice a night. I gravitated to the position because it allowed me considerable free time to embark on another career direction that had long intrigued me—that of a fiction writer.

Drawing from my experiences as a newspaperman, I was relatively quickly able to place short stories with magazines like *Liberty* and *Saturday Evening Post*, and then began work on a novel. It was a good life. From my radio duties, the bills were paid and the remainder of my time I could spend being truly creative—something every newsman longs for.

Most important, my conscience was clear. Since I had total control over how and what I reported to my listening public, I no longer had to worry about career damaging stories like the Taylor affair. Never again would I, through innuendo, badger an unfortunate like Mabel Normand. Although I reported the straight facts on my broadcasts, I went out of my way to make sure the public wouldn't draw any wrong conclusions—at least from my coverage. Indeed, there were times when, convinced that a newspaper was wrongly persecuting an individual, I would editorialize against my own colleagues' methods. My new policy made me both friends and enemies.

The *Dispatch* died a year after I departed its ranks. Evidently, readers didn't appreciate the new "yellow" tinge, nor did advertisers. Both disappeared rather rapidly after Austin took charge. Its playboy publisher, not wishing to pump money into an unprofitable venture (his fortune had already been considerably eroded by the crash), shuttered the sheet in May of 1933. The building that housed the once admired paper was razed in 1952 in favor of a parking lot.

24

It was a series of civil actions involving Charlotte Shelby that brought about the final (such as it was) denouement of the William Desmond Taylor murder case. The first of these came about in 1933 when Mama filed suit, in the amount of $200,000, against Leslie B. Henry, her securities broker, and the firm for which he worked, Blythe and Company.

Henry, a personable gentleman and one-time chairman of the Pasadena Tournament of Roses, had been convicted of grand theft of more than $40,000 from Mrs. Shelby, although *she* claimed he'd stolen nearly $500,000 from the securities account she had entrusted to him. $400,000 of the money was supposed to have belonged to Mary.

The broker replied that he'd performed services for Mrs. Shelby for many months without recompense, was entrusted with many valuable secrets, and when he received no payment from the matron and was in a financially precarious position himself, he had used some of her money for investment, intending to return it to her account. Henry went to prison, protesting that Mrs. Shelby knew about these questionable actions all along.

The attorney for the brokerage house answered that his firm wasn't responsible for Henry's actions, which he considered were part of their personal relationship: "*The mother and the agent, Les Henry, entered into an alliance to keep the little actress* (Mary Minter) *in poverty. Up to the time she became of age, Mary turned over all her earnings to Mrs. Shelby. After she became of age, her mother signed a contract with her through which she was to receive thirty percent of Mary's earnings.*

"The fact was that Mary was allowed nothing while her sister Margaret had everything. Mary was violently unhappy during those years, for her mother and her sister were always accusing her of terrible things and desiring intimacies with men, and keeping her indebted to them at all times."

August 30, 1935, Charlotte Shelby again sued Blythe—this time for $500,000. She asserted that during the 1933 action, Henry and his employer had libelously linked her name with the Taylor murder, although that case had nothing to do with the one at issue, and that course was taken purely to humiliate and embarrass her.

Henry, said the complaint, falsely stated in his deposition that she was fearful of being indicted for the slaying by then District Attorney Asa Keyes when he was on his widely publicized 1926 national tour, ostensibly investigating the Los Angeles killing. Prior to her departure to Europe, Henry allegedly claimed that she'd said, "Well, they will have to find me if you get word to me that the indictment has come."

Always one to dote on press coverage, Mrs. Shelby commented on her relationship with Henry, who was then residing in San Quentin prison: *"I know, of course, that he was stealing the money and not putting it into securities. It was simply blackmail because he threatened that if I questioned his activities he could bring about my indictment for the murder of William Desmond Taylor whenever he wanted to.*

"I do not expect to get the money back. I am sure he has dissipated all of it. I am bringing this suit so I can air out in open court all this suspicion, all these rumors that everybody seems to believe, that I shot Mr. Taylor."

Unfortunately for her, the case never went to trial, having been dropped somewhere along the way, and the charges never got their public airing.

On February 2, 1937—the fifteenth anniversary of the discovery of Taylor's body—two significant events took place in the offices of D.A. Burton Fitts. A graying Mrs. Ada Deane-Tanner, wife of the late director's long missing brother, Dennis Deane-Tanner (declared legally dead in 1924) appeared on the scene to inform the prosecutor she wished to *"clear my husband's name of the stigma placed against it."*

In her possession were three faded documents, two envelopes and a letter, each one in the handwriting of Dennis. It was her hope that, compared against verified samples of Edward Sands' handwriting that were on file, police experts could disprove the prevailing fifteen-year-old hypothesis that Dennis and the valet were one and the same person. This theory, of course, stemmed from an anonymous letter, postmarked from Denver, which had suggested the relationship, claiming that Dennis harbored a grudge against his brother as a result of a boyhood quarrel over a girl.

Fitts directed the documents turned over to James Clark Sellers, internationally known handwriting expert, for a microscopic examination. Sellers' conclusion: *"I am unable to find any handwriting characteristics which would even suggest that Deane-Tanner and Edward F. Sands were the same writer."*

And thus, one aspect of the mystery was cleared up at last. Whoever Sands was, he *wasn't* Taylor's brother, Dennis.

The other visitor Fitts had that day was Mary Miles Minter, angered at a recent news story that resurrected the memory of the nightgown found in Taylor's quarters, which some reporters claimed bore her initials. The garment, she said, had been the single material object that stood between her and total vindication in the murder. In fact, Mary asserted, it never actually existed in the first place. Taking a lesson in tactics from her mother, she demanded that the district attorney either try her for Taylor's murder or, failing that, clear her in a public statement.

Fitts, who had never seen the nightgown himself, sent an aide to fetch it, but word soon came back that neither it, nor nothing like it, was in the police evidence room. The next day, he told the press that Mary had been absolved of any suspicion in the case, adding that so far as *his* office was concerned, she had never been under suspicion.

Twenty-four hours after that, he made another, rather unexpected announcement. He said that "CLOSED" had been written across files in the case. Death had ended it, because Edward Sands *"is dead."*

"*Shortly after the murder of Mr. Taylor,*" continued the prosecutor, "*a complaint was issued against Sands, charging him with that murder. He was never apprehended. In so far as exhibits and physical evidence in the case are concerned, my office has at no time possessed such evidence.*"

What brought about this sudden "closing" of the Taylor case? Another six months would go by before I learned the answer.

Actually, the files didn't stay closed for long. The month of May brought the biggest surprise the case had produced since the discovery of Mary Minter's love letters in 1922. The "zinger" came in the form of a statement given by Margaret Shelby Fillmore in a deposition she'd made during the course of a lawsuit against her mother.

Like her sister Mary, Margaret spent much of the 1920s and 1930s battling with Charlotte Shelby both in and out of court. She'd married Hugh Hamilton Fillmore, grandson of the President, but the union did not last. Among her neighbors in the fashionable Laguna Beach community in which she resided, the eldest Shelby girl was known as an alcoholic.

At one point in their disputes, Margaret threw Mama and all her belongings out of the house, whereupon the older woman phoned press photographers and, sitting forlornly on her luggage stacked on the sidewalk, gladly posed for them. Later, Mrs. Shelby attempted to have her daughter committed to a mental institution, but the court dismissed her complaint. It was Margaret's anger at this unsuccessful attempt on her mother's part that motivated her to file the new lawsuit.

Margaret contended in her suit that Charlotte owed her $48,000—the balance due on an original debt of $133,000 owed her since 1923. To support her case, the daughter's attorney, Clyde Murphy, took her sworn deposition. The answers he and opposing counsel received were definitely more than they'd bargained for:

Mrs. Shelby's lawyer in cross-examination: *Was Mrs. Shelby under any legal or moral obligation to you in the year 1923 to give you $133,000?*

Margaret: *The moral obligation would have been a matter of opinion, but it was more or less to stand by her against the public; staying by her and walking the floor with Thomas Lee Woolwine; keeping her out of more possible consequences.*

Lawyer: *You feel your services in that regard was reasonably worth $133,000?*

Margaret: *If I had been in that position, I would have paid my last cent for shielding.*

Lawyer: *Was Mrs. Shelby under accusation at that time?*

Margaret: *Some people thought so.*

Lawyer: *And for that service you charged the modest sum of $133,000. What did you give your mother in return for that agreement?*

Margaret: *Do you want me to speak frankly?*

Lawyer: *Yes.*

Margaret: *I protected her against the Taylor murder case.*

Lawyer: *Is it your contention that your mother killed William Desmond Taylor?*

Margaret: *I don't have an answer for that.*

And, she didn't. By utilizing what might have been *planned* innuendoes, Mrs. Fillmore had all but accused her mother of the murder.

This information, as well as Margaret's further revelations that her sister kept a secret diary, was enough to convince Clyde Murphy to send a copy of the deposition to Burton Fitts who, in turn, instructed his assistant, Eugene Williams, to take the case before the Grand Jury.

Charlotte Shelby made another of her public statements, again welcoming the opportunity to clear herself in a public hearing. She also, somewhere along the line, related a strange episode of gunplay in her youngest daughter's home. Mary, back in 1922, was supposed to have, following a family disagreement, gone to her room and fired a shot. The actress laughed when the panicked family rushed in.

Acting on orders from the district attorney, police went to Miss Minter's house and, brandishing a search warrant, seized the diaries Margaret had mentioned.

I hadn't covered a news story in years, but in this case, nothing was going to keep me away from that Grand Jury hearing. As with all judicial sessions of this type, neither the press nor the public were allowed access to the hearing itself. However, much could be gleaned by observing and talking to the witnesses, both before and after their testimony.

The three witnesses (Mrs. Shelby and her daughters) arrived outside the Grand Jury room at almost the same time. Mary, carrying more weight than she'd ever exhibited before, greeted her mother affectionately, then both she and Charlotte attempted, without success, to speak with Mrs. Fillmore.

"Hello, my Margaret," Mrs. Shelby said as her eldest child passed close to her. The mother tried to take her arm, but the girl jerked it away and did not reply, appearing not to notice her sister.

Margaret was the first to be called and, following two hours of questioning in the secret session, she emerged weeping, only to be whisked away by her attorney. Later, we learned that she told the Jury about a love affair between her sister and former actor/director James Kirkwood. In 1916, when Miss Minter was fifteen years old, she and the performer were supposed to have motored to Santa Barbara and strolled together through the fields. Kirkwood was said to have placed the teenager on a rock, knelt before her and declaimed: "I, James, take you Mary for my wife in the sight of God."

Speaking from his home in Grand Rapids, Michigan, Kirkwood expressed total ignorance of the alleged incident, although he did admit that he'd directed Miss Minter in some films. Burton Fitts, subsequently, made it clear that Kirkwood was in no way implicated in the murder.

Miss Minter was the second to be interrogated by the Jury. Afterwards, she told the reporters that her diaries were of no importance to the case: "*They did mention William Desmond Taylor. I was seventeen and loved him dearly. We were engaged. It is the great tragedy of my life that he never lived to be my husband.*

"*One of those diaries stopped two years before his death. The other starts about two weeks afterward, and it isn't exactly a diary. When the shock began to wear off, I started to write about how much I missed him and about how I loved him. It was more a record of my emotions and sensations at that time than a day-to-day log of my comings and goings.*"

Fitts would agree with Miss Minter that the diaries proved to be utterly useless in the case. "*It had been previously reported to my office,*" he explained, "*that these diaries held the secret of the Taylor killing.*"

To protect the former actress' interests, exact contents of the diaries were never made public.

While her daughters were being questioned, Charlotte Shelby made a statement: "*I am delighted that Mr. Fitts responded so quickly to my request for the investigation of the Taylor murder case. For the past fifteen years, there have been many rumors circulated on innumerable fronts against me. Now comes practically a formal charge by my own daughter, Mrs. Margaret Shelby Fillmore, to the effect that I withheld important facts and she assisted me in withholding them from the authorities. If she or any other person has any other facts concerning the murder of William Desmond Taylor, I demand that they be disclosed immediately.*

"*Unfortunately, my daughter, Mrs. Fillmore, is very bitter against me because circumstances last summer forced me to take rather drastic steps for my daughter's own good.*" (She was referring, of course, to the unsuccessful insanity complaint she'd filed.)

Upon completion of Mrs. Shelby's testimony, a barrage of questions were leveled at her.

"I was asked," she said, "if I'd shot Mr. Taylor or if I knew who did. I said 'No' to both questions."

"What about Margaret's charges against you?" I inquired.

"They didn't even question me about what Margaret told them, whatever it was."

Then she offered: "They asked me if I ever owned a gun. I told them I had. It was a little thing, practically a toy, given to me by Mr. Eaves." (Harry Eaves, it was learned, was a Santa Barbara jeweler.)

"I only shot it once while he was teaching me how to handle it. I haven't the slightest idea what became of it."

Deputy D.A. Eugene Williams said that his detectives would find out. He added, "For the first time in a number of years, the Taylor file is nearly complete."

That was it. No further action was ever taken on the case. Sure, there was another "wild goose chase" down in Mexico in search of Edward Sands and, a few months after that, Margaret Fillmore claimed her grandmother, Julia Miles, had disposed of the murder weapon in a Louisiana bayou. But, for all practical purposes, the police and district attorney had washed their hands of the matter.

25

I wasn't satisfied. For fifteen years, I'd followed the progress, or lack thereof, in the Taylor murder. Indeed, I'd almost lost my life that night on College Street. No way would I let this thing rest without some sort of explanation.

As far as I was concerned, everything—or, at least, many elements—seemed to fit now. The blonde hairs found on the body; the nightgown; the monogrammed undergarments snatched by Ike St. Johns, who'd died in 1935 from heart failure; those childish love letters of Mary Minter's, not to mention her own statements about her and her mother's true feelings about William Desmond Taylor, certainly made a convincing argument that Charlotte Shelby had a strong motive to "do in" the director.

Then, there was my gut feeling that Faith Cole MacLean did, indeed, recognize her "mysterious stranger." The comedian's wife definitely knew Mary Miles Minter's mother on sight.

Whether Charles Eyton and the other Lasky executives at the time knew the answer to the mystery, I wasn't sure. If they did, protecting Mary Minter's $2 million name from scandal was good enough reason for refusing to cooperate fully with either press or authorities. Conversely, other picture folk who may have learned or suspected the killer's identity might have kept silent to avoid hurting the sweet innocent Mary—even though they may have disliked her mother.

This was all theory on my part, but considering statements made in the Les Henry/Blythe matter and admissions during the past few months by Margaret Fillmore, I couldn't understand why Fitts hadn't indicted Charlotte Shelby, or at the very least explained his failure to do so.

City Hall was well aware of my radio editorials, so when I phoned Deputy D.A. Eugene Williams' office, he granted me an immediate interview. This capable attorney later gained fame following World War II as the prosecutor of Japanese war criminals.

A patient man, he listened attentively to my case, then after lighting his pipe, told me what I'd waited so long to hear. "First thing you must realize, Mr. Birnbaum," he said, "is that everything I tell you must be off-the-record. This conversation never took place. Any conclusions you draw from it are strictly for your own edification. Agreed?"

"I never expected to use this," I nodded. "Agreed."

"Your argument is certainly a logical one, but I'm not going to comment—one way or the other—as to whether I agree with you or not."

"Will you tell me, at least, why you haven't filed an indictment in this case?"

"Be glad to. We have no physical evidence." He saw my mouth start to open in protest, but stopped me. "Back in February, when Mr. Fitts announced that the nightgown was not in the evidence room, he didn't tell everything. Also absent were the 'blonde hairs' and a few other miscellaneous pieces of evidence."

"What became of them?"

"We're not sure," he said. "They were inventoried back in 1922. There's no question about that. But, a couple of years later these items were checked out and, according to records, never returned."

"Who checked them out?"

"Thomas Lee Woolwine."

Williams gave me a few moments to recover from this unbelievable disclosure before he continued. "Mr. Fitts and I don't know the answers to your obvious questions. We've pondered them ourselves."

"You must have a theory."

"Just conjecture. But, let's look at your hypothesis for a moment. Let's just pretend *for argument's sake* that your theory about Charlotte Shelby is absolutely correct. This is just conjecture, mind you."

Knowing full well his true meaning, I said that I understood.

"Given that Woolwine knew everything that you've suggested," reasoned Williams, "what might he have done?"

"You're the lawyer," I replied.

"Based on the physical evidence we logged in, he could have probably made a reasonable case that Mary Minter was having an affair with Taylor. Right? That would have, at least, established a motive for Mrs. Shelby.

"But, the only thing he had to tie the mother to the crime itself was the testimony of Mrs. MacLean, who said that the party leaving the bungalow *could* have been a woman. If she later specifically named Charlotte Shelby as that person, I don't know about it, because part of her written statement is missing from the files.

"That, in a nutshell, was Woolwine's entire case. He was a sharp enough prosecutor to know that an amateur defense attorney would take that case apart. There was no way he could convict that woman."

"Explain."

"First, it was dark outside when Mrs. MacLean saw the 'killer.' No matter how positive she might sound on the witness stand, the jury is going to discount her testimony.

"Secondly, a reasonable case can also be made against Edward Sands, the valet, or that narcotics peddlers were responsible."

"And what of the motive?" I asked.

"It's self-defeating. What 1922 jury would have convicted a mother for shooting the dirty old man who had debauched her young daughter? Would you?"

I saw his point. "But why would Woolwine remove the evidence?" I asked.

"I don't know. I understand he was a great believer in Western justice. Maybe he felt that Charlotte Shelby was morally right in protecting her daughter and, when he left office, decided to ensure that no succeeding administration—like this one, for example—would prosecute the woman for what he considered to be a just act."

Finished with his argument, Williams got up and walked toward the door—a signal that he wished to terminate the interview. "Again,

I emphasize," he said, "that everything I've just said is strictly conjecture. I don't know who *really* killed William Desmond Taylor."

Rising from my chair, I tendered, "What about the Grand Jury testimony?"

"It produced nothing conclusive. Margaret Fillmore is not the most reliable witness and Mrs. Shelby certainly didn't confess."

"So, that's it?" I said. "The case is really closed?"

"It remains 'unsolved.' But, don't be too disappointed. If you're truly convinced that Mrs. Shelby is the guilty party, then you've got to believe in Divine retribution.

"Look at her life since the murder. The career that she worked so hard to build for Mary was destroyed; she lost a good deal of her money in that Leslie Henry securities theft; and she definitely doesn't have the best relationship with her daughters. Guilty or not, that woman has been punished."

Shaking hands, he decided to leave me with one parting thought, "Remember, as far as this office is concerned, we don't know who committed the murder."

Al Drebin and I met for lunch that noon in a coffee shop across from the *Times* building. He didn't seem surprised at what had transpired between Williams and me.

"I'll tell you something else," he said, "also off the record. In fact, there are only three or four officers in the department who know about this at all.

"Remember Mrs. Shelby's story about Mary going up to her bedroom and shooting off a gun?"

I nodded.

"A couple of guys in homicide got the idea of going over to that house—the one on Fremont Place—and trying to recover that slug, assuming it exists in the first place."

That was one hell of an idea. If it could be shown through ballistics that the bullet came from the same gun that killed Taylor, then the case against Charlotte Shelby would virtually be open and shut.

Al proceeded with his story. "Some sort of X-ray scanning device was borrowed from Lockheed Aircraft," he said, "and we got permission by letter from the house's new owners to go up to Mary's old room and see what we could find.

"It could very well have been a large nail, but the boys reported back that, within the wall, there appeared to be a metal object that *could* possibly be a bullet."

"Why didn't you try to recover it?"

"The owners were in Europe and the caretaker wasn't about to let us rip any walls out. So, we decided to try for a court order."

"And. . ."

"Before we had a chance to do anything, orders came from 'upstairs' to forget about it. The department was having budget problems, so it was decided to put the investigators on a more current case.

"I was furious, but what could I do?"

Al could see that I was also getting angry at this indifference on the part of the L.A.P.D. "Relax, Ben-a-la," he shrugged, "be realistic and roll with it."

"How can you say that?" I demanded. "You've been on this case just as long as I have."

"The world's changing," reasoned Al. "New people are murdered every day. If I *did* solve the Taylor case now, it would simply be an academic exercise. Who would really give a damn?"

I hated to admit it, but he was right.

The William Desmond Taylor murder is, today, but a faint memory. Although mystery buffs rank it alongside the "Black Dahlia" and the disappearance of Judge Crater as being one of the country's most baffling unresolved crimes of the 20th century, this case and the Arbuckle scandal are together relegated to a single sentence in the *Encyclopedia Britannica*'s description of the early days of Hollywood and the establishment of the Hays Office.

Yet, it was events such as the Taylor/Arbuckle episodes and the subsequent formation of the regulatory agency that were to have a profound effect on the motion picture industry for decades to come. Once talking pictures became a reality, the Hays Office formulated its strict Production Code—outlining what producers could and could not do on the screen. These puritanical rules prevailed within the film capital until a relatively few years ago when a new generation of creative personnel, armed with recent Supreme Court decisions on the First Amendment, confirmed an almost "anything goes" policy as far as how and what movies could deal with—and thereby put an end to the Taylor/Arbuckle legacy.

The cast of characters who played out the Taylor drama are gone. Alcoholic and virtually friendless, Margaret Shelby Fillmore died in 1939, leaving her small estate to her housekeeper—a bequest that both Charlotte Shelby and Mary Minter took to court to dispute.

Mrs. Shelby finally reconciled with her youngest daughter, who'd reverted to her legal name, Juliet Shelby. In 1956, the two women requested the Superior Court to terminate a $100,000 trust fund established by Charlotte in 1924, with some of her daughter's film earnings for the benefit of the former actress. Mary told the court that the funds in the trust were now needed "for necessities of life."

Charlotte Shelby succumbed on March 13, 1957, in her daughter's Santa Monica home. Carl Stockdale, her alibi witness for the night of the murder, passed two days later. As a character actor, he had successfully transitioned from silent films to sound and remained active into the 1940s. Whether he was telling the truth about that night is open to speculation, but the fact that he continued to work fairly regularly, unlike other performers connected with the case whose careers were destroyed or virtually ended with the coming of sound, makes me wonder if the studios, or somebody, appreciated that he was a "good soldier" and didn't rock the boat.

Death took Faith Cole MacLean in 1959.

Mary Miles Minter finally married in 1957. The groom was real estate developer Brandon O'Hildebrandt, a Danish-American and a friend of the silent film star for many years. He died on August 13, 1965.

The portly widow continued to reside in Santa Monica with a housekeeper/companion. Those who knew her would not recognize her as the golden curled girl who once rivaled the screen popularity of Mary Pickford.

On impulse, in the late 1970s, I phoned her one evening, thinking I might get her to chat about the Taylor case. Her husky voice surprised me, but she was cautiously friendly. About the only thing she did say about the murder was that she thought Edward Sands did it, and that I should refer to the victim as "Mr. Taylor."

Mary Miles Minter died on August 4, 1984.

Al Drebin is also dead. He passed away in 1961—the victim of stomach cancer.

As for myself, I really have no complaints with life. I continued my radio program until 1951, at which time I retired to do nothing but write. Over the years, I've established myself as a commercial writer of light fiction. No best sellers, but the quantity of my submissions have provided Carol and me with a comfortable income.

Just before World War II, I bought about thirty acres of land in the wilds of the San Fernando Valley. Carol thought I was nuts speculating with $5,000 like that, but she bowed to my "superior business judgment." I sold the same property ten years ago to a shopping center developer. That handsome profit paid for our six month tour of Europe and the Orient, and has provided us with the means to live the rest of our lives out very handsomely in Newport Beach.

My son, Joshua, became an accountant; served as a captain in the European campaign; married a beautiful girl and had two children; and is now a grandfather himself. The entire family lives in the Los Angeles/Orange County area and we all get together several times a year.

So, why have I waited so long before writing about the Taylor case?

My colleagues in the writing game tell me that it's not easy to put down on paper a story that you've actually lived—especially one containing so many diverse elements that, had I not seen it happen first hand, I wouldn't believe myself.

Nevertheless, since I've reached the age where one's days are numbered, the realization came that, if this fascinating story was ever to be documented by one who didn't have to rely on old newspaper clippings and history books to get his information, then I'd better get to work *fast*.

Whenever I'm in the Wilshire District of Los Angeles, I make it a point to drive by the house at 56 Fremont Place to see if it's still standing. More than once, I've been tempted to go up to the door and, if I could convince the resident that I wasn't crazy, offer them money to let me go upstairs and punch a hole in a bedroom wall.

But, I always suppress the desire. Maybe I'm afraid that the bullet won't match the one still held in the dark recesses of the L.A.P.D. evidence room or, even worse, perhaps there's nothing in the wall at all.

As we all know, maintaining a fantasy is sometimes much more pleasant than facing reality.

Hollywood Memorial Park on Santa Monica Blvd. is well-known for the famous personages who rest there under lavishly designed monuments—Douglas Fairbanks, Cecil B. DeMille, and Tyrone Power come to mind almost immediately, as does the name of Rudolph Valentino, who is the subject of an annual ceremony held in the Cathedral Mausoleum.

Down the aisle from Valentino's resting place is vault #594. Attached to the white marble exterior is a bronze plaque, bearing the inscription: "In Memory of William C. Deane-Tanner, Beloved Father of Ethel D. Deanne-Tanner. Died February 1, 1922."

Few who pass this spot are aware that the world knew Mr. Tanner as William Desmond Taylor, respected motion picture director. As far as the official records are concerned, his murder remains "unsolved."

But, is it?

Benjamin A. Birnbaum
(1895-1987)

Afterword

Who killed William Desmond Taylor?

Most likely, it was Charlotte Shelby.

That is certainly the most popular solution offered by the many authors who have written about this still officially unsolved case.

Yes, it could have been Edward Sands, or a drug dealer, or even Mary Miles Minter, but I'm with the majority on this one. It was probably Mary's mama.

The truth is that we are never going to know for sure who pulled the trigger on Bill that fateful night. All anybody can do is speculate.

I'd first heard about the Taylor mystery when I was about nine or ten years old. Somewhere I had viewed a one or two-reel comedy starring Mabel Normand and, as I recall, my mother mentioned that Mabel had been involved in a sensational murder case. But, I didn't take a serious interest in Taylor until the mid-1970s. I had already written several books about Hollywood, its movies and personalities, and I was anxious to branch out; perhaps write a novel based on a true crime story.

With my ongoing interest in Hollywood and its history, I was soon attracted to the complex murder mystery of William Desmond Taylor and the wealth of colorful characters who populated the story. I submerged myself in research, reading virtually every book and newspaper article that dealt with the case, even those that were obviously false leads or red herrings. I interviewed people who were still around from that turbulent time, including legendary newspaperwoman Adela Rogers St. Johns, directors King Vidor, and Allan Dwan, Actor Keye Luke, who provided me with a lucid portrait of Los Angeles' Chinatown of the early 1920s, and I even had a phone interview with Mary Miles Minter.

I don't recall exactly why, but at some point during that period, the Taylor project went on a back shelf and I never really returned to it. My guess is that some paid writing assignments, probably my Charlton Heston and Merv Griffin books, came along at that time, and they took precedence over a project I was doing on spec.

Let's jump ahead almost forty years. I always wanted to write something about the Taylor case, but never had. I'm sure that the 1986 publication of Sidney D. Kirkpatrick's excellent book, *A Cast of Killers*, was a factor in my not returning to my project, yet I always felt a little guilty about letting all my research go to waste.

Recently, I came up with a concept that would allow me to adapt the Taylor saga into a stage play, so I pulled out my box of research materials on the case, which had been in my storage space until about six months ago, and got a shock.

Inside the box was the completed manuscript of the novel based on fact that you have just read. Truthfully, I had totally forgotten that I even wrote it. There were plenty of handwritten corrections and notes on the typewritten pages, which is probably another reason why I never returned to finish it. Nobody really had a home computer back in the mid-1970s, and to get the manuscript ready for publication I would have had to retype the entire thing. I guess I didn't have the time, or the desire to do that.

The manuscript needed some tidying up and, as Mary Miles Minter, as well as my other sources, had passed away since I'd written it, a bit of updating.

Aside from Kirkpatrick's, there have been other books published on the Taylor murder during the past four decades. I haven't read any of those others, but I do believe that *Murder in Babylon* is the only book that looks at the case from the day-to-day viewpoint of a newspaperman, albeit fictional, who was covering it. Ben Birnbaum, Al Drebin, and a few other characters may be products of this author's imagination, but the facts of the case itself, including the false leads and red herrings, are taken from the newspaper reports of the time, as well as information supplied by my interview sources.

I hope you enjoyed reading it.

Michael B. Druxman
September 8, 2014

About the Author

Michael B. Druxman is a veteran Hollywood screenwriter whose credits include *Cheyenne Warrior* with Kelly Preston; *Dillinger and Capone* starring Martin Sheen and F. Murray Abraham; and *The Doorway* with Roy Scheider, which he also directed.

He is also a prolific playwright, his one-person plays, *Jolson* and *Lombard* having had numerous productions around the country. Other produced stage credits include one-person plays about Clark Gable, Spencer Tracy, and Orson Welles. These and plays about Errol Flynn, Basil Rathbone, Jeanette MacDonald and Nelson Eddy, Maurice Chevalier, and Clara Bow have been individually published under the collective title of *The Hollywood Legends*. An eleventh play in the collection, *B Movie*, deals with the Franchot Tone/Barbara Payton/Tom Neal scandal of the 1950s.

Additionally, Mr. Druxman is the author of more than fifteen other published books, including several nonfiction works about Hollywood, its movies, and the people who make them (e.g., *Basil Rathbone: His Life and His Films*; *Make It Again, Sam: A Survey of Movie Remakes*; *One Good Film Deserves Another: A Survey of Movie Sequels*; *Merv* [Griffin]; and *The Musical: From Broadway to Hollywood*).

He has written two prior novels, *Nobody Drowns in Mineral Lake* and *Shadow Watcher*, a book of short stories entitled *Dracula Meet Jack the Ripper & Other Revisionist Histories*, plus the humorous revisionist history, *Once Upon a Time in Hollywood: From the Secret Files of Harry Pennypacker*, and *Family Secret*, a non-fiction book co-authored with Warren Hull which reveals the true facts behind the 1947 murder of mobster "Bugsy" Siegel in Beverly Hills.

An acknowledged Hollywood historian, he has also written television documentaries and has been interviewed for various retrospective featurettes that have accompanied DVD releases of classic films (e.g. *The Maltese Falcon*, etc.).

Mr. Druxman is a former Hollywood publicist with thirty-five years of experience who has represented many film and television stars, as well as noted directors, producers and composers. One of his Academy Award campaigns is often mentioned in books dealing with Oscar's history.

He has taught various dramatic writing and film appreciation courses at an adult university and is the author of *How to Write a Story... Any Story: The Art of Storytelling*, which has been used as a text in several colleges. He is often invited to speak to groups of aspiring film and television professionals to discuss screenwriting and the realities of show business.

A native of Seattle who graduated from Garfield High School and the University of Washington, Mr. Druxman moved with his wife, Sandy, from Los Angeles to Austin, TX in 2009.

His two memoirs, *My Forty-Five Years in Hollywood and How I Escaped Alive* and *Life, Liberty, and the Pursuit of Hollywood* are both published by BearManor Media.

www.ingramcontent.com/pod-product-compliance
Lightning Source LLC
Chambersburg PA
CBHW071838020726
47502CB00004B/1410